EAGLESMOUNT

the Silver horn

The Eaglesmount Trilogy

THE SILVER HORN

THE EMERALD THRONE

THE LAKE OF DARKNESS

EAGLESMOUNT

The Silver horn

Cherith Baldry
Illustrated by David Wyatt

Hardcover edition first published in the United States in 2002 by MONDO Publishing,
by arrangement with Macmillan Children's Books, 25 Ecclestone Place, London SW1W 9NF

Text copyright © 2001 by Cherith Baldry
Illustrations copyright © 2001 by David Wyatt

For information contact:
MONDO Publishing
980 Avenue of the Americas
New York, NY 10018
Visit our website at www.mondopub.com

Printed in the United States of America

02 03 04 05 06 07 08 HC 9 8 7 6 5 4 3 2 1
09 10 11 12 PB 9 8 7 6 5 4 3 2

ISBN 1-59034-475-8 (hc)   1-59034-490-1 (pb)

Originally published in London in 2001 by Macmillan Children's Books.
Typesetting and cover design for this edition by Symon Chow.

Library of Congress Cataloging-in-Publication Data

Baldry, Cherith
The Silver Horn / Cherith Baldry ; illustrated by David Wyatt
p. cm.
The first book in the Eaglesmount trilogy, followed by "The Emerald Throne"
and "The Lake of Darkness".
Summary: Vair, a brave young pine marten, had hoped to show off his skill
with a sword at the Watersmeet summer fair, but after his father is killed by
a gang of thieves, Vair learns that his destiny will take him to Watersmeet
for a more important reason.
    ISBN 1-59034-475-8 -- ISBN 1-59034-490-1 (pbk. : alk. paper)
    [1. Animals--Fiction. 2. Fantasy.] I. Title: Eaglesmount. II. Wyatt,
David, ill. III. Title.

PZ7.B18175 Si 2002
[Fic]--dc21   2002029503

To Helen

Prologue

Long ago, in the land of Riverbourne, the eagles ruled. Theirs was a fair and happy land, but their rule was destined not to last. In the reign of King Aquila the Nineteenth, a darkness rose out of Dernwater. Night covered the sun; sleet fell in summer and beat down the standing corn.

Mustering his eagle warriors, King Aquila took wing and led them to Dernwater, the lake that we now call Owlswater. Guessing that he flew to his last battle, he foretold that one day, after long years, an heir would arise and restore the land to the glory that was passing.

Above the lake King Aquila joined in combat against a vast black dragon, whose breath seared the forest and turned the village of Colthwaite to a ruin. Long and hard they fought, for a day and a night, until King Aquila and his followers defeated the dragon and drove it into the lake to drown.

The noble-hearted eagles paid a great price for their victory. Exhausted, wounded to death, they fell from the sky, and none of them ever returned to the heights of Eaglesmount. The line of the High Kings was at an end.

In great sorrow the falcon stewards of the kingdom vowed to preserve the memory of the eagles and write down all they had achieved. Then Wayland, the badgersmith, wrought a silver horn, and carved upon it the words of King Aquila's prophecy. So that the heir to the royal eagles might be recognized, he crafted the horn so that none but the true heir could sound it.

All this was done, and the courts of Eaglesmount were left empty until the heir should come. But as years went by, the silver horn was lost, and no one knew what had become of it.

– Gurman, *A History of Riverbourne*, Ch. 14

Triumph

Vair gripped the hilt of his sword. He was a young pine marten with a strong, lithe body and fur the color of a glossy chestnut. His eyes were bright and watchful.

Warily he began to circle the forest clearing, looking for the chance to attack. His opponent, a pine marten like himself, was older, and the scars in his thick brown fur showed that he was a veteran of many fights.

Sunlight danced through the trees and flashed on the blade of Vair's sword. Birds sang in the branches, and not far away, Vair could hear the soft gurgle of a stream. The air carried the scents of early summer.

Suddenly the peace was shattered as Vair's opponent darted forward, striking low to get under Vair's guard. Vair blocked and the swords clashed together. For a moment Vair stood face to face with his attacker and caught the gleam of delight in the older pine marten's eyes. Then he sprang back, disengaging the blades.

The older animal was laughing. Forgetting caution, Vair hurled himself forward, his sword slashing back and forth in a flurry of blows. His opponent gave ground, and Vair thought he might be able to drive him back against the trunk of a huge oak tree that stood at one side of the clearing, but at the last moment, the other pine marten slipped aside and aimed a stroke at Vair's hindpaws.

Vair leapt over the blade, but now he found he was the one pinned against the tree.

"Had enough?" his opponent said, grinning.

"No!" Vair growled.

Grimly Vair forced his way forward again, beating his attacker's blade aside. Step by step he pushed out into the center of the clearing. Sweat was starting to trickle through his fur and into his eyes, and his breath was becoming short.

"You're not fit, lad," his opponent taunted him.

He raised his sword for a massive downstroke. Vair launched himself toward it. With a twist of his own blade, he caught it near the hilt, and it went spinning out of his opponent's paw, away into the undergrowth.

With a yell of triumph, Vair tossed his own sword aside and flung himself on the older pine marten, bearing him backwards onto the moss. His paws

fastened in the creamy fur at his opponent's throat.

"Now who's not fit?" he asked through bared teeth.

The older pine marten was laughing. He grabbed Vair and hugged him, and then he tried to shove him away. "Get off, you big lump. What about a bit of respect for your poor old father?"

"Poor old father?" Vair scrambled to his hindpaws and reached down to help his father up. "That's the first time you've let me get anywhere near you."

Vair's father, Sandor, rested his paws on Vair's shoulders and looked him in the eye. "I didn't let you, son. You won that bout fair and square. If I didn't think you'd get bigheaded, I'd tell you that you've the makings of the finest sword fighter I've ever seen—and I've seen a few."

Vair felt a surge of pride. "Do you really think so?"

"I do. You've learned well. But just one thing—if you're fighting, really fighting for your life, don't let your enemy make you angry. That's when you make mistakes." He stretched, and winced. "I'll be stiff tomorrow. Come on, it's time we were going. Your mother'll wonder what's happened to us."

Sandor walked off towards the stream, while Vair collected the swords and followed him.

When Vair caught up with Sandor, his father was kneeling beside the pool at the foot of a small waterfall, hauling up a fish trap. Sandor tossed three good-sized trout onto the grass and killed them swiftly with his belt knife, while Vair released a few smaller fish back into the stream. Vair watched them swim away until they were lost to sight among the drifting weeds in deep pools shaded by overhanging branches.

Vair let out a sigh. It was hard to believe that this tiny stream came spilling out of Coolspring, the mountain lake where Vair and his family had their home, and grew until it became a river, the mighty Spine, that ran through the whole country of Riverbourne as far as the distant sea.

"I've been thinking . . ." Vair said.

"Hmm?" Sandor tossed his catch into a basket and pulled a wisp of grass to clean the blade of his belt knife. "Thinking what?"

"When you were my age, you traveled all over the world. You've told us about sailing ships and pirates, and . . . I've never been or seen anywhere, except here."

Sandor looked around him, with a contented smile on his face. "You'll go a long way, lad, before you see anything finer than this." He raised a paw as Vair started to protest. "But you're young. You see things differently. I know."

"I don't want to leave," Vair said. "Not for good. But I want . . ."

"All right, lad. Spit it out."

"I wondered . . . couldn't we go to Watersmeet, to the Midsummer Fair? We could travel by boat nearly all the way. It wouldn't be hard. And I was thinking . . ." He hesitated, a bit embarrassed to be putting his dreams into words. "They have contests there, don't they? For archery and swordplay? I want to enter. I want to see if I'm really any good!"

Sandor grinned at him. "Oh, so that's it! Well . . . " He stood up, sheathed his belt knife and his sword, and slung the basket of fish over one shoulder. "We'll see. Let's ask your mother what she thinks about it."

He turned upstream along the faint trail by the

waterside, and Vair followed him joyfully. He imagined he could hear the cheering and applause of the crowds at the Watersmeet Midsummer Fair as he vanquished his opponent and won the prize. Then he shook his head self-consciously. Whatever Sandor said, Vair didn't really think he would be able to defeat the best fighters in the country. It would be enough to take part and hope for enough success to make Sandor proud of him.

The sun was going down by the time Vair and Sandor reached the spreading beech tree where they made their home. As Sandor lifted the latch of the door in the trunk, Vair could hear his mother Riska humming a tune. She was lighting the lamps in the big room between the tree roots.

"Fish for supper!" Sandor called.

The humming went on, but there was an excited squeal and Vair's little brother Cuffi hurtled into the hall and flung himself at his father. Sandor laughed and handed the basket to Vair so he could haul the cub up onto his shoulder.

Vair's mother dusted off her paws when she had finished lighting the last of the earthenware lamps. Then she took the fish into the kitchen and began to clean them expertly. Vair set the table, while his sister, Mirra, filled a dish with nuts and dried crab apple slices from the cupboard.

Soon the family was sitting down to a supper of fried trout, clover, and chestnut bread.

"Listen, all of you," Sandor said. "Vair here wants us to go to the Watersmeet Midsummer Fair. What do you think?"

Mirra's eyes were sparkling with excitement, and Cuffi started jigging up and down in his chair and squeaking, "Watersmeet! Watersmeet!"

His mother hushed him. Laying down her knife and fork, she said, "I don't know. Only this morning Mistress Sainfoin told me she's heard there are bandits roaming the woods. I don't think it's a good time to travel."

"Oh, Mother!" said Mirra, disappointed.

"All rabbits gossip," said Sandor bluntly. "And Mistress Sainfoin is one of the worst. I haven't heard anything about bandits."

"If there's trouble, Father and I can fight," said Vair.

"And me!" Cuffi added, slashing his knife back and forth as if it were a sword. "I'll get all the bandits!"

"That's quite enough from you," Riska said as she took hold of Cuffi's knife and set it on the table.

"Remember, there'll be lots of other animals going to Watersmeet," Sandor said. "Once we get as far as Acornbury, we can join a bigger party. That'll make any bandits think twice."

"Please, Mother!" said Vair.

Riska hesitated, and then she smiled. "Well . . . you'll all give me no peace until I say yes."

"You mean we can go?" Mirra asked.

"I suppose so," Riska sighed.

Cuffi let out a shriek of excitement and bounced in his chair, waving his paws around and almost knocking over his mug of elderflower cordial. Vair had to laugh at his little brother's antics, but at the same time, he couldn't help noticing that his mother still looked faintly worried.

As he got up to close the shutters against the gathering night outside, he heard in the distance the repeated calling of an owl.

Cap'n Ragnar

Sandor blew on the pile of twigs and dried leaves, and a flame flickered upwards into the evening air. He gave a grunt of satisfaction and fed the fire carefully with more twigs. "Soon be ready," he said.

Vair crouched down beside the heap of wood he had gathered and watched his father. The third day of their journey was coming to an end. Nothing had spoiled the peace of the woodlands as they traveled downstream. Tomorrow they would reach the thriving village of Acornbury, where they were bound to fall in with other animals making their way to Watersmeet. Vair had been watchful ever since they left home, but now he started to relax.

Once the fire was burning merrily, Sandor set up a forked stick on either side of it and balanced a third stick across the flames. On the balance stick were a couple of plump trout that Vair and Mirra had caught in the stream. Sandor had cleaned them and stuffed them with freshly picked herbs. As they started to sizzle, Vair sniffed the delicious smell and remembered how hungry he was.

Sandor had built the fire on a flat, pebbly stretch of ground beside the stream. Further up the bank, Riska was spreading out their bedrolls, helped by Cuffi, who kept diving underneath them and growling, pretending to be a bear.

Suddenly Riska straightened up. "Shh! I thought I heard something."

At first, Vair could hear nothing except the gentle gurgling of the stream and the faint sighing of wind in

the branches. Then he began to make out the crashing of heavy hindpaws through the undergrowth, as if a large group of animals were making their way through the woods.

The sound grew louder as they approached. In the gathering twilight Vair could see nothing at first. Then the bushes beneath the trees parted, and the first of the newcomers stepped into the circle of firelight. He was an enormous silver fox, dressed in a grubby velvet coat that had once been scarlet and was trimmed with tarnished gold braids. More animals crowded up behind him as he stopped, with one forepaw on the hilt of the sword in his belt.

Vair sprang to his hindpaws. Beside him, his father remained crouched over the fire. "Greetings, friends," said Sandor. "What can we do for you?"

The fox grinned and gave Sandor a mocking bow. "Glad you remember your manners, pine marten," he said. "What can you do for us? Well, we'll take supper with you for a start, and then we'll see."

"You're welcome to share our fire," said Sandor steadily. "But if you want fish, you'll have to catch your own."

"Hear that, lads?" The fox glanced over his shoulder at the band of animals behind him. "That's not friendly, not friendly at all. I reckon we'll have to teach him a lesson."

"Aye, Cap'n Ragnar." The animal who spoke was the biggest ferret Vair had ever seen, with sharp, uneven teeth and wicked eyes. He drew his sword and stepped forward beside the fox.

For a moment Vair stood frozen. He saw his mother stoop to gather up Cuffi in one arm, while with her free forepaw she gripped the long knife Sandor had used to clean the fish. Mirra drew closer to her side.

At the same time, Sandor threw himself backwards and grabbed his sword from where it was lying on the bank close by. "Vair!" he called.

Vair caught his own sword as Sandor tossed it to him and faced Captain Ragnar and his crew. The fox was still grinning. "Oh, fierce pine martens," he said. "I reckon that just makes it more fun, don't you, lads?"

There was a chorus of "Aye, Cap'n!"

The fox drew his sword and took a step forward. Vair braced himself, knowing that he and his father were hopelessly outnumbered by the ragged group of bandits who stood menacingly before them.

Sandor grabbed a blazing branch from the fire and hurled it in Ragnar's face. The fox ducked, and the branch whirled over his head, but a howl from somewhere behind Ragnar told Vair that one of his crew hadn't dodged quickly enough.

The bandits surged forward. Vair ran to meet them. A ragged stoat rushed at him, yelling and waving his sword.

Vair felt the shock as his own sword clashed against the blade. He sprang back and slashed. The stoat's yells turned into a gurgling cry, and he fell backwards.

Not waiting to see what had happened to the ragged stoat, Vair spun around, sword gripped in both paws as he looked for his next attacker. The branch Sandor hurled had set fire to the bushes, and smoke was billowing over the campsite.

Vair couldn't see his father, but he heard him shouting, "No, Riska! Don't fight, run! We'll hold them off—get the young ones out of here!"

Coughing in the smoke, Vair stumbled toward his father's voice, but the dark shape that loomed up in front of him was not Sandor. Vair recognized the ferret and barely brought his sword around in time to stop the sword of the huge creature. The force of the blow jarred his whole body.

The ferret was grinning. "That's right, little marten," he said. "I likes a good fight."

Vair slashed at him, but the stroke missed. He saw flame reflected on the ferret's blade and felt it slice into his shoulder and across his chest. He sprang backwards. He could see his own blood, bright red where it spattered over his shirt, dark where it soaked his fur.

He did not feel much pain. He only knew that he had to stay on his hindpaws and hold back the ferret until his mother and the children had time to escape.

He lifted the sword for another stroke, but the blade felt very heavy.

The ferret was closing in on him. He was grinning, his eyes gleaming in triumph. Then the triumph turned to a snarl of rage as Vair managed to bring his sword down and gash the ferret's leg down to the hindpaw.

Howling in fury, the ferret stumbled but kept on coming. Vair backed away, hoping for a tree he could lean against to guard his back while he fought on as long as he could. Smoke and sweat were blurring his eyes; the smell of blood and fire was in his nostrils. He swung his sword once more, but he could feel himself weakening. The ferret beat the blade aside.

As Vair braced himself for the blow he knew was coming, his hindpaw caught on something. Off balance, he staggered backwards and fell. Pain stabbed through his head. He lost his grip on his sword. He tried to get up and roll away from the attack. As he put weight on his forepaw, the pain of his wound surged through him.

He made one more effort to rise and thought he heard the ferret's laughter. His limbs would not obey him. He could do no more; darkness was rising all around him. He felt a faint regret; he would never be able to tell Sandor that he had done his best. Then he let himself slip down into the darkness.

Captain Ragnar's Servant

Vair opened his eyes. He was lying on the moss under the trees. Night had fallen, and the forest was strangely quiet.

At first he did not remember what had happened. Then, as he tried to sit up, he felt pain in his wounded shoulder, and his head swam from loss of blood. He could see burnt-out bracken and smell the acrid smoke that still curled sluggishly upwards from the blackened bushes where Sandor's burning branch had fallen.

Wondering if any of his family were close enough to hear him, he took a breath to call out but stopped himself before he made a sound. He did not know what had happened to the bandits; they might still be close by.

For a few moments, he sat with his head in his paws, trying to find the strength to get up. He was desperately thirsty. He wanted a drink, and he wanted the pain to stop.

When he finally struggled to his hindpaws, he caught sight of a gleam of firelight from further downstream. He began to stumble toward it when a burst of raucous laughter reached him, and he realized that the bandits were seated around the campfire that Sandor had built.

He half turned, uncertain of what to do, and almost fell over the body of a stoat, lying on its back with a snarl frozen on its face. He recognized it as the one he had killed himself. Vair skirted it cautiously. He knew he had to get closer to the fire to see if any of his family were prisoners. As he reached the next clump of bushes, he stopped, with his paws pressed to his mouth to stop himself from being sick.

Between the bushes and the bank of the stream Sandor lay on his back. His fur was soaked with blood. Forcing himself to move, Vair stumbled forward, stooped over his father, and reached out to him, desperately seeking a heartbeat. He could feel nothing. Sandor was dead, but he had taken three of the bandits with him.

Blindly Vair turned away and fell to his knees by the waterside. He scooped up the cold water in his paws, gulped mouthfuls of it, and splashed it over his face and neck until his head started to clear and he could think again.

He stripped off his torn, filthy shirt and ripped it

into strips. Clumsily, one-pawed, he bathed his wound and fastened a bandage around it.

Then he went back to his father. For a few moments he looked down at him, remembering all the fun and laughter they had shared when Vair himself had been a cub as young as Cuffi, and thinking about how much he had learned from Sandor as he grew up. He knew that he had to be strong—that he had to look after his mother and the little ones.

He took Sandor's sword from his paw and stood with it for a moment over his father's body. "I'll find the others. I promise," he said. "I'll make sure they're safe."

With the sword gripped tightly in his paw, he crept downstream toward the campfire. By the firelight Vair could see Ragnar sitting with a mug in one paw. Beside him was the ferret Vair had wounded, with a bandage on his leg and hindpaw, and four others, a stoat and three rats. They had opened his family's knapsacks and were stuffing themselves with the food Riska had packed for the journey.

Vair knew there were far too many for him to fight. What he needed to do was discover whether his mother or the children were prisoners, and if they were, he had to find some way of releasing them without alerting the fox and his crew.

He slid silently through the bushes until he was

close enough to hear what they were saying.

"Good grub, Cap'n," one of the rats mumbled through a mouthful of Riska's barley bread.

"Aye," Ragnar said genially. "You stick with Captain Ragnar, and I'll see you're fed right. This is a good country, a soft country, and we're going to live off it. We can take what we want, because there isn't anybody brave enough to stop us. Are you with me, lads?"

There were shouts of "Aye!" and "All the way, Cap'n!"

The stoat, who was sitting a little apart from the others nursing a burnt shoulder, said, "Won't they have warriors to fight us, Cap'n?"

"Warriors!" Ragnar spat into the fire. "They're soft, I tell you. Fat from too much good living."

"Like the pine marten you killed?" the stoat asked. "He weren't fat, or soft, Cap'n. He killed my best mate."

"Ketch," Ragnar's voice was suddenly so soft that Vair could scarcely hear it, "you're not losing your nerve, are you? You're not thinking of running out on me? Because I wouldn't like that, Ketch. I wouldn't like it at all."

"No, Cap'n!" The stoat sounded frightened now. "I wouldn't do that, Cap'n, not for nothing."

Vair had heard enough. He couldn't see his family,

and he began to hope that they had escaped. What he had to do was follow them.

He wormed his way away from the fire and toward the place where he had last seen his mother and the young ones, near the bedrolls that were still spread out on the ground away from the stream.

Just beyond them, Vair could see a place where the bracken was broken down, a dark hollow leading into the woods, as if someone had fled that way.

His hopes rose higher, and he hurried toward it, leaving the fire and the bandits behind him.

As he paused on the edge of the trees, something sharp pricked the back of his neck. He froze.

A voice said, "And where was you a-going?"

A paw gripped his arm and spun him round. Vair found himself face-to-face with a grinning stoat, with a sword in his other paw. Pain surged through him again as he struggled. He tried to raise Sandor's sword, but the stoat batted it out of his paw as carelessly as swatting a fly. He released Vair while he picked it up, but Vair could only sway on his hindpaws, too weak to take the chance of running.

The stoat jerked his head towards the campfire. "Move."

He followed Vair, prodding him in the back with his sword point as Vair stumbled toward the fire. As they reached the circle of firelight, the stoat said, "Look what I got, Cap'n."

The silver fox was cleaning his claws with a dagger. As Vair appeared he looked up and sounded bored as he said to the ferret, "Gorm, I thought you told me this one was dead?"

"He was dead, Cap'n Ragnar," the ferret said. "Dead and done for." His face split into an evil, snaggletoothed grin. "I can kill him again for you, Cap'n. No trouble."

"Maybe. Maybe not." Captain Ragnar looked Vair up and down. "He just might be more useful alive. What's your name, scum?"

"I won't tell you!" Vair spat at him. "You can't make me."

"Oh, I can, if I want to. Gorm is good at finding out things, aren't you, Gorm? You'd best be polite, little scum, or I might let Gorm have his fun with you."

"Do you think I care?" Vair's head was reeling with pain and exhaustion. He knew he had to stay angry, or he would break down and weep in front of them all. "You killed my father."

The fox gave a mocking grin. "And what are you going to do about it, little scum? Challenge me to single combat? I'm shaking in my boots."

Vair was silent.

Ragnar laughed. "See?" he said to his crew. "Soft, like I said."

"Let me have him, Cap'n," the big ferret said hungrily.

"Oh, no," said Ragnar. "This one's mine. It's high time I had a servant."

"I won't serve you!" said Vair.

Ragnar shot out a paw, grabbed Vair by his creamy neck fur, and pulled him close. With the other paw he rested the point of his dagger at Vair's throat. "Scum," he said, "you'll do what I tell you."

Vair wanted to shout defiance into Ragnar's sneering face. He would have died willingly if he could have killed Ragnar and taken revenge for Sandor's death. But even more than that, he wanted to find his

31

mother and Mirra and Cuffi, and for that he had to stay alive. He tried to shrink away, pretending to be afraid.

"Don't—don't kill me, Captain," he said. "All right, I'll serve you. I'll do anything you want."

Ragnar released him with a mocking laugh. "Build up the fire, then. And get our beds ready. We need a good night's sleep, don't we, lads? We've got an important appointment tomorrow."

As Vair dragged branches from the woodpile to the fire, he couldn't help wondering what the appointment was and what other villainy the silver fox was plotting.

The Meeting

The following morning the bandits packed up their camp and trekked through the belt of woodland alongside the stream, heading east for the open fields beyond. Trudging along, shoulders bowed under a heavy pack, Vair was in too much pain to ask himself where they were going. He needed all his strength just to stay on his hindpaws.

Once they left the trees behind, the land grew bleak and barren. There was no shelter from the hot sun. Vair panted in the heat; his mouth was parched with thirst. He began to feel that he could not go on putting one hindpaw in front of the other, but if he stumbled, the huge ferret Gorm was there behind him, prodding at him with Sandor's sword to make him keep going.

Vair felt hot with anger to see his father's sword in the evil creature's paw. He promised himself revenge, but he could not see any hope of taking it. His wound had weakened him, and there were too many bandits for him to tackle alone. He could not even hope for escape.

Pictures of his mother and his brother and sister kept flickering in front of his eyes. Sometimes he saw them returning to the campsite and finding Sandor's body. Sometimes they were fleeing through the woods, calling to him and weeping when he did not answer. Sometimes—worst of all—they were lying dead like Sandor. Vair wondered if he would ever find out what had happened to them.

The bandits took a short rest at midday and then tramped on into the hills. They saw no other creatures until the sun was setting. Then Vair heard the sound of raucous singing, and a column of weasels came into view, plodding single file across the crest of the hill.

Ragnar hailed them. "Greetings, Grim! What news?"

The head weasel halted, and his followers shuffled to a stop behind him. "Ragnar! Might have known you would be here."

The silver fox laughed. "No need to be unfriendly, Grim. There'll be loot enough for all of us."

"That's as may be," the weasel grunted. "Just stay out of my way, Ragnar, and I'll stay out of yours."

He set off again, the bandits jostling and snarling as the two groups tried to follow the same trail. When they had settled down again, Vair realized that Ragnar had taken the lead, while Grim and the other weasels trudged along behind.

Soon they came to the crest of the hill. Through eyes blurred with weariness, Vair looked down at the dark line of the pine forest that licked up the slopes on the far side.

Inglewood. He had never seen it before, but he had heard stories about it. Exciting stories, when you were sitting safe at home with a bright fire and a good stout door between you and the night. Vair didn't think the stories were so exciting as he gazed down at the forest and saw the sun sinking behind it.

Among the pine trees Vair caught glimpses of a lake that was the color of blood in the last rays of sunlight—Owlswater. The stories they told about Owlswater were worse than the stories they told about the forest. No one went near it, except for the owls it was named for. Surely Ragnar didn't mean to go there!

The silver fox turned to march along the ridge. They had not gone much further when Vair began to hear noise from up ahead: voices and the sound of a large number of creatures moving around. He realized they must be close to the meeting place Ragnar was heading for.

The silver fox led the way to a jagged outcrop of rocks standing in a rough circle and pushed his way through a gap. Vair heard him call out a greeting and the chorus of groans and yells that answered it. Vair stepped between the rocks in his turn and looked down.

Vair stood on the lip of a bowl-shaped dip in the ground. Rocks surrounded it, and a single tall rock stood upright in the center. The sides of the bowl were lined with fierce creatures. Vair stared down at a forest of bright eyes, sharp teeth and claws, and the glint of weapons.

Grinning broadly, Ragnar led his band down the side of the bowl to a place near the center. Other creatures made way for him, and he saluted them as he passed and sat down in a space near the central rock.

At last Vair was able to drop his pack and sink down on the turf beside it. The sudden relief from its weight made his head swim, but he forced himself to sit up and look around.

Leaning against the central rock was a wolf. He wore a black shirt and tight-fitting black britches that outlined every muscle of his lean, gray body. His muzzle was scarred, and he wore a black patch over his left eye. A slender sword hung at his hip. His booted hindpaws were crossed at the ankles, and his arms were folded. He stared out over the heads of the bandits as if they bored him.

The bandits were passing around food and drink, talking among themselves or yelling insults at enemies. A few more came in over the lip of the bowl and found themselves places. The wolf ignored them all, and as the light died Vair realized that everyone was waiting.

The darkness grew, a few stars appeared in the sky, and the moon lifted above the rocks. Then soundlessly, like a ghost out of the night, a pale blur of wings swooped over the crowd of bandits, who ducked their heads and cried out in alarm. Vair crouched down as he caught a glimpse of crooked talons. It was an owl, gliding down to the top of the central rock, where he perched and gazed at those gathered around him. The bandits fell silent as the fierce eyes raked over them.

Vair caught his breath as he stared at the creature. He had never seen an owl as big or as terrifying as this. His underside was pale, but his back and wings were a dark chestnut color, feathered with black. Even in the darkness, his eyes glared amber. Vair shrank against the pack he had carried and hoped the owl would not notice one insignificant pine marten.

The wolf drew his sword and raised it in a salute. "Greetings, Lord Owl!" His voice was clipped and gravelly, but it carried to every part of the bowl. "Your servants are assembled."

"So I see," the owl hissed. "Listen, vermin. Under the moon just past, I sent out my messengers to find those of your kind and appoint this meeting place. Now the time has come for me to tell you why I have summoned you. I have a task for you. A task that will bring you rich rewards."

Someone among the bandits, bolder than the others, called out, "What task is that, then?"

"And what reward?" That was Ragnar; the silver fox got to his hindpaws and bowed. "Tell us, Lord Owl, what's in it for us?"

The owl's great head came swivelling around, as he fixed his glaring amber eyes on Ragnar.

"Enough," he said. "Enough even to satisfy you, fox. Be silent and listen. This little country has no king. The animals live in villages. They are stupid enough to think they can rule themselves." He let out a hiss of contempt. "Soon they will learn better. I, the Lord Owl, intend to rule here in Riverbourne. I will crush them under my talons and make them my slaves."

"So what do you want with us?" Grim the weasel asked. The huge bird turned his head and fixed the weasel with his stare. "Sorry, great Lord Owl," Grim added hurriedly.

"You will be my advance guard," the Lord Owl explained. "Each group of you choose a village and move in. Make yourselves at home. Terrify the wretched creatures who live there. Teach them obedience. Then when I come, they will be too weak and frightened to resist me."

"I still don't see what's in it for us," Ragnar said, still on his hindpaws. "Begging your pardon, Lord Owl, but why should we do your dirty work for you?"

The Lord Owl let out a long, furious hiss. "Fool!" he said. "All the plunder of the village you choose will be yours. And you shall be its lord when I am king."

Ragnar put one paw on his chest and made an even more elaborate bow to the Lord Owl. Vair thought he could see fear underneath his swagger. "Fair enough, Lord Owl," he said, "but me and my lads could take that anyway. Why shouldn't we?"

Behind Ragnar, the stoat Ketch muttered, "Stow it, Cap'n. That bird could rip yer liver out!"

Vair wouldn't have been surprised to see the Lord Owl attack Ragnar, but instead it was the wolf who intervened in a lazy drawl that had a hint of a snarl in it.

"Believe me, my friend, you don't want to know what will happen if you annoy the Lord Owl."

Panic-stricken, Ketch tugged at Ragnar's coat to make him sit down and be quiet. Ragnar shoved him away angrily, but he squatted on the ground again.

"Very well," the Lord Owl said. "The meeting is over. Go where you please—except for one village. Do not go to Watersmeet. I have other plans for Watersmeet. And remember that I shall be watching."

A low muttering spread around the bowl, gradually growing louder and more excited. Some of the animals started to leave, as if they couldn't even wait for daylight. Or perhaps, Vair thought, they just wanted to be out of the way of the Lord Owl.

Ragnar, however, beckoned his crew into a huddle around him. "I reckon that mangy bird's out of his mind," he said, but Vair noticed that he glanced over his shoulder to make sure the Lord Owl was not listening before he spoke. "Making himself king! I never heard such rubbish! But listen to me." The rats and stoats leaned even closer, while Gorm the ferret listened with a gap-toothed grin. "We'll do what he says. Why not, when there's riches in this country, just lying around waiting for us to pick 'em up?"

"What riches, Cap'n?" one of the rats asked, staring vacantly around.

"Good food and drink, fool," said Ragnar. "Fine clothes and soft beds in snug houses. Soft, stupid animals to wait on us. Here for the taking, like the Lord Owl said. What more could an animal want?"

He sprang to his hindpaws. "Listen, lads—" he began to say and then broke off with a gurgling sound in his throat as the wolf stepped softly over the turf behind him, spun him around, and buried his sword point in the fur at his throat. In the darkness and the confusion as the bandits left the bowl, Ragnar's crew had not seen the wolf approach.

"Fox," he said softly, "you talk too much. Come and speak to the Lord Owl."

Ragnar tried to look around for help without moving his head, but his own gang were frozen with fear, and the remaining bandits were scrambling away as fast as they could.

"All right," Ragnar said hoarsely as the wolf dropped his sword point. "No need to be nasty."

The wolf held his sword at the ready as he followed Ragnar across the turf to the base of the central rock where the Lord Owl still perched. Vair and Ragnar's band stayed where they were, crouched watching on the ground nearby. Silence fell as the last of the departing bandits vanished between the rocks on the lip of the bowl. Clouds drifted across the moon; Ragnar and the Lord Owl were bathed in shifting light and darkness.

The Lord Owl held Ragnar for a long time in his compelling gaze. Vair was surprised when he said at last, "I like you, fox. I like an animal who would double-cross his own grandmother." He stared down into Ragnar's eyes, and his voice grew softer. "Just so long as you don't cross me."

Ragnar cleared his throat. "Not a chance, great

Lord Owl."

"Will you swear an oath to serve me? I need an animal I can trust for a special mission," Lord Owl continued.

For a moment Vair thought Ragnar was undecided. He glanced from side to side, as if he was looking for a way of escape, but the Lord Owl was poised to strike at him, his wings half extended, his cruel beak curving down toward the fox's eyes. The wolf lounged against the rock again, sighting down the blade of his sword. Gorm and the rest of Ragnar's band were too scared to back him up.

Ragnar drew himself to his full height. "I will, lord."

"Kneel, then," Lord Owl commanded.

Vair guessed that any oath Ragnar swore would last as long as the Lord Owl could see him. He wondered why the Lord Owl didn't realize that. Then as the Lord Owl spread his wings above the kneeling Ragnar, as if he would swoop down on him, Vair began to sense something in the darkness outside the bowl.

He could see nothing, but he felt such a powerful surge of menace that he wanted to flatten himself on the turf and whimper like a cub having a nightmare. Something—perhaps the night itself—was pressing in around them. The silver crescent of the moon, riding high in the sky, had turned to a dusky gold, as if a dark mist was cutting off its light. Vair wondered if Ragnar

43

and the others could feel the evil as he did.

The Lord Owl spoke, his voice ringing around the hollow. "Repeat these words, 'I swear to follow the Lord Owl . . .'"

"I swear to follow the Lord Owl . . ." Ragnar's voice was shaking. ". . . to be his creature . . . to aid him in word and deed . . . and to take him for my king."

When the oath was over, Vair thought the evil presence outside the ring of rocks retreated a little. He began to relax and realized that he was shivering.

"It is well." The Lord Owl settled back on the rock. His head swivelled around to gaze at the wolf. "Konrad, give him his orders."

"Well, fox," the wolf drawled, "how do you feel about a little trip to Watersmeet?"

"You told us to stay away from Watersmeet," Ragnar said.

"And now we tell you to go there. Somewhere in Watersmeet, fox, there is a horn. A silver horn, engraved with strange markings. Find it, and bring it to the Lord Owl. When you do so, he will not be ungrateful. Fail and . . ." He gave a shrug and flicked his sword point across Ragnar's chest. "I suggest you try very hard not to fail."

44

Watersmeet

Kyria hummed a tune as she stirred the pot on her kitchen stove. She was a young vixen with glossy red-brown fur and a sharp, intelligent face. Today, for the messy jobs in the kitchen, she was wearing an old brown frock with the sleeves rolled up and an apron over it.

Some of the villagers, Kyria knew, thought that she sang charms over her cures, but today she sang because the sun was shining on Watersmeet, and in a few days, the Midsummer Fair would begin.

Leaving the pot to simmer, she began to check the earthenware jars of herbs and ointments that lined one wall of her kitchen. She had spent the last few weeks gathering, drying, and blending her healing herbs and potions, and she wanted to be sure everything was ready.

The kitchen door opened, and her father, Flick,

came in, coughing and flapping a paw in front of his face.

"What have you got in there?" he asked. "I could smell it all the way from the Merry Ferret."

"Wild thyme cordial," Kyria replied. "And if you've been in the Merry Ferret, you'd better have some, or you'll have a headache tomorrow."

She took down Flick's silver drinking horn from the shelf, ladled some of the cordial into it, and set it in its wooden stand on the table beside her father.

Flick chuckled. "I've just been recruiting Wiggin as a Deputy Warden. Got to make sure everything runs smoothly when the fair starts."

Kyria sniffed. She couldn't help thinking that the preparations for the fair were a good excuse for Flick, the Warden of Watersmeet, and Wiggin, the innkeeper of the Merry Ferret, to get together and sample Wiggin's famous Barley Brew.

Flick picked up the silver horn, blew on the hot cordial, and took a cautious sip. "Wiggin thinks he might run short of elderberry wine for the Fair Feast," he said. "He told me to ask you if you can let him have an extra cask."

"I might." Kyria went back to the kitchen range, gave the pot another stir, and drew it aside to cool. "There. That's done. I'll go down and talk to Wiggin now."

"Do that." Flick grinned. "You'll find your friend Flora there. She just arrived."

"Flora! Why didn't you say so?" Kyria whipped off her apron, wiped her paws on it, and tossed it into the washing basket. "I'll be back later."

"Don't stay there gossiping and forget my supper," said Flick.

Kyria gazed at her father narrowly to make sure he was joking. "Gossip!" she said. "Huh! If I'm not back in time, you can make your own supper." She went out, banging the kitchen door behind her.

The home that Kyria shared with her father was built into the side of the hill that sloped gently up from the Broad River. The path into the center of the village led along the waterside. Sunlight sparkled off the shallow water gurgling contentedly along the riverbed.

Swallows darted across the sky above Kyria's head as she walked along the path. She raised a paw to wave, but they took no notice of her. Swallows, she thought, were a scatterbrained lot.

The Merry Ferret Inn was built on a spit of land that jutted out at the point where the Broad River met the Spine. Just before the two rivers joined was a wooden landing stage, where a couple of boats were tied up. Kyria climbed the steps cut into the bank.

On her way up, she paused to look downstream.

From here, the view stretched past the meeting of the two rivers and down the Spine as far as the northern end of Winding Lake, which was lost in the blue distance. A white-and-gold paddle steamer was tied up at the lakehead jetty. Kyria wasn't sure that she trusted a boat that went without wind or oars against the current, and the Whiteport animals, who owned it, didn't often come so far north. Still, she knew no harm of them. Everyone was welcome in Watersmeet at the Midsummer Fair.

As she climbed the rest of the steps, she began to hear the sound of singing. Reaching the village green, she wasn't surprised to see the choir, lined up in the shade of a silver birch tree and practicing the music for the Fair Feast. They were mostly young, a collection of water voles, rabbits, and hedgehogs, with a single badger at the back, and they were standing up straight and singing with great enthusiasm to make up for what they lacked in tunefulness.

Shadow, the red squirrel who was the choir organizer, was conducting using his flute as a baton.

"No, no, *no*," he said as Kyria paused to listen. "That's B flat, not B natural. Here, you, vole, what'syourname, where's your music?"

The singing came to a ragged halt. The young vole Shadow had spoken to wiped his nose on his paw. He muttered, "Forgot it."

"Forgot it? Agh!" Shadow clutched his fur. "How can you expect to sing if you forget the music? *All* right!" He waved the flute again. "From the top. One and two and three and—hedgehog on the end there! Are you *eating*?"

The hedgehog, whom Kyria recognized as one of Wiggin's enormous brood, swallowed hastily and fixed Shadow with an innocent stare. "Eating? Me?"

Two rabbit girls in identical pink flouncy frocks looked at each other and giggled.

"I give up," said Shadow. "I do. I give up. Go away, the lot of you. Same time tomorrow. And remember the music next time!" he called as the young animals scattered.

When they had gone, he strolled over to join Kyria. He was not much older than most of his choir, and he was grinning cheerfully. "They'll be fine on the night," he promised.

"You always say that."

"I'm always right, too."

Kyria sniffed. Actually, he was right, but she was not going to admit it to him.

Shadow fell into step beside her as she walked across to the Merry Ferret. The old inn was a rambling building made out of logs, with a roof that might have been thatched to begin with, but now was almost covered with moss, grasses, and all manner of

49

wildflowers. The lines of the windows and the door were crooked, as if over the years the inn had settled comfortably into the ground. As well as the rooms in the building itself, there were more rooms and cellars dug into the bank below, with windows looking over the river. There were even rooms in the enormous chestnut tree that spread its branches over the inn. Not many creatures would fail to find somewhere that suited them at the Merry Ferret.

In front of the inn, bordering the village green, were several tables. At the one nearest Kyria, three otters from the Whiteport paddle steamer were sitting, crisp and smart in their white uniforms. They nodded in a friendly way to Kyria and Shadow as they walked past.

Wiggin, the innkeeper, was spreading red-and-white checked cloths over the tables, but he stopped what he was doing as Kyria and Shadow approached.

"Have you seen your dad, Miss Kyria?" he asked.

"Yes, he asked me about the wine. That's fine, Wiggin, if you can send somebody to fetch it. Is one cask enough?" Kyria asked smiling.

The plump hedgehog scratched his spines. "I'd not say no to two. Get this lot 'round a table, and—"

"Kyria Flicksdaughter!" A cheerful bellow drowned out what the innkeeper was saying. "Have ye never a word for your old friend?"

At the end table, an enormous wildcat was sprawled

50

on the bench. She wore brightly checked trousers tucked into her boots and a checked cloak fastened at the shoulder over a white linen shirt. There was a sword at her side, and the hilt of a dagger poked out of the top of her boot. A mug of Barley Brew was on the table in front of her.

"Flora MacStripe!" said Kyria.

As she hurried to greet her friend, the wildcat sprang up, striped fur rippling, and enveloped her in a hug. "Ye're a sight for sore eyes," she said. "And ye, wee tree-rat," she added to Shadow, fetching him such a slap on the back that he staggered to keep his balance. "Still singing?"

"Still singing," Shadow gasped. "And don't call me tree-rat."

"It's good to be back," Flora said. She slapped the hilt of her sword. "Will we be having a practice bout, Kyria?"

"Maybe later," Kyria said.

"Later might be too late," said the wildcat, with a sudden frown.

"What do you mean?" asked Kyria.

"Bandits," said Flora. "There's bandits in the hills. Maybe ye'd better be watching out for trouble, Kyria."

Kyria laughed, though she noticed that Shadow was looking anxious. "Oh, Flora, there are always stories!" she said. "The Midsummer Fair has been held in

Watersmeet for years, and there's never more trouble than Flick can handle."

The huge wildcat was still frowning. "It's more than stories, Kyria. I met with some of them on my way down from the north." She breathed on her claws and buffed them against her checked cloak. "There's not so many of them now, though."

"I still think—" Kyria began.

"Kyria, look!" Shadow interrupted her.

He was pointing towards the upper landing stage on the Spine. Flora swung around, and her paw went to the hilt of her sword. Kyria drew in her breath sharply.

Across the village green, a silver fox in a grubby scarlet coat came swaggering, followed by a crew of dangerous-looking rats and stoats and a huge ferret. Trailing behind them, weighed down by a heavy bundle, was a bedraggled pine marten.

"Kyria," Shadow said nervously, "I think Flora might be right."

Unwelcome Guests

Vair staggered up the path from the landing stage under the weight of Ragnar's pack. His wound was throbbing painfully, and he felt extremely tired. But he was in Watersmeet at last.

To the right of the path was a raised bank with doors and windows set into it. As Ragnar passed, a window flew open, and an elderly rabbit appeared, shaking a duster. When she saw the bandits, she stared open-mouthed and then slammed the window shut. Vair felt hot with shame.

The path wound up from the river to the village green. A ring of trees surrounded it: tall elms and beeches and chestnuts. The ground was covered with smooth turf, starred with daisies. Vair could see that animals made their homes in the trees. Washing was strung from branch to branch, here and there a rope ladder dangled down, and enticing smells of cooking wafted through the air.

Along one side of the green, tables were set out in front of a comfortable old inn. Ragnar strode across the grass toward it, followed by his crew, with Vair bringing up the rear.

A group of otters was seated at one of the tables, and other animals stood watching as Ragnar led the way toward them. Vair couldn't help staring at the enormous wildcat in checked trousers and cloak. Ragnar had said all the villagers were soft and stupid, but this creature looked more than a match for him.

Beside her stood a young vixen, a red squirrel, and a plump old hedgehog with a towel over one arm. Their faces showed a mixture of fear and hostility as Ragnar's band drew closer. Vair felt that look like another wound. They would see him with Ragnar and think he was a bandit like the rest of them. They would never be his friends.

Ragnar reached the inn and flung himself into a seat at one of the tables. The rest of his crew crowded around, while Vair dropped his pack on the grass and squatted down beside it, hoping no one would notice him.

"Landlord!" Ragnar bellowed, pounding the table. "Fetch us ale!"

The old hedgehog began ambling slowly across to Ragnar's table.

"And look sharp about it, fool!" Ragnar ordered.

The hedgehog didn't move any faster. He smiled and nodded as he reached the table, and smoothed down the towel he carried.

"Good afternoon, gentlebeasts," he said. "Welcome to Watersmeet. I'm Wiggin, the innkeeper here. What can I do for you?"

"You heard me," Ragnar snapped. "Fetch us ale. Or are you deaf as well as stupid?"

"Ale it is, sir." Wiggin still spoke mildly, though his smile had vanished. "And will you be wanting supper later? I've a fine pike roasting, with fennel and—"

So quickly that Vair didn't see the movement, Ragnar pulled out his belt knife and plunged the blade into the wooden table top, through the cloth. "Ale," he said through his teeth. "*Now!* Move!"

"There's no call for that," Wiggin said.

At the same moment the huge wildcat put her paw on her sword hilt and stepped forward.

The vixen grabbed her arm. "No, Flora!"

"I'll not let that lout do as he likes," the wildcat said. "My flesh and blood can't stand it, Kyria."

"But we can't have fighting, just before the fair," the vixen said desperately. "You know Flick wouldn't like it."

"Maybe." The wildcat's voice was a low growl, but she let Kyria draw her to one side.

"Now listen," Ragnar said, leaning across the table toward Wiggin. "Innkeeper—Wiggle or whatever your name is. I'm Captain Ragnar, and when I tell you to do something, you do it. Right?"

Wiggin hesitated, glanced uncertainly around the ring of fierce animals, and then looked back at Ragnar. "Right. Ale coming up, sir," he said, and vanished into the inn.

Kyria turned to the red squirrel and said so softly that Vair only just heard her, "Shadow, go and fetch Flick."

Immediately the red squirrel bounded off around the corner of the inn. Vair thought he looked glad to go.

Ragnar leaned back in his seat, wrenched his dagger out of the table top, and started tossing it up into the air and catching it by the hilt. Vair could see he was in a good mood, now that he had upset everyone and made them do what he wanted.

Soon Wiggin came back, carrying a tray with a jug and several mugs. Ragnar poured ale for himself, and then the rest of his band fought and jostled, spilling the ale as they splashed it into their mugs.

Vair buried his head in his paws, wishing he could be anywhere but here. No one in Watersmeet would welcome him now. His dream was spoiled, and he was no closer to finding his mother and the young ones.

Instead, he was Ragnar's prisoner, mixed up in the evil plots of the Lord Owl and his search for the mysterious silver horn.

A cry from Kyria made him look up again. Egged on by the other bandits, Ketch the stoat had unslung the crossbow on his back and was sighting at the table where the three otters were sitting. The otters dived for cover, pulling their table over with them.

Vair could not just sit there and watch. He stumbled to his hindpaws and made a grab for Ketch, only to jerk to a halt as Ragnar gripped his wounded shoulder.

"Keep out of this, scum." The silver fox gave him a stinging blow across the side of the head. "Let Ketch have his fun."

Vair collapsed on the ground again, dazed with pain. Meanwhile, Kyria leapt for Ketch's bow and managed to knock it upwards. The bolt went high, burying itself in the thatched roof of the Merry Ferret. Ketch turned on her, snarling a curse.

The vixen had her paw on her belt knife when Flora shouldered her way between her friend and the stoat.

"Have ye nothing else to be doing, laddie?" she asked. "Or will I be wrapping your bowstring 'round your neck?"

Vair almost felt like laughing at Ketch's face, frozen with fear, as he scuttled backwards, out of range of Flora's teeth and claws. He shoved his way

in among the rest of the band, grabbing at his mug of ale and burying his snout in it as the others poked fun at him.

The otters were setting their table upright again when Vair saw the red squirrel reappear from beyond the inn. An old fox was with him. He looked so much like the young vixen that Vair guessed they were father and daughter.

The fox strode up to the table where Ragnar sat and tapped him on the shoulder. "Captain Ragnar? What's going on here?" he asked.

Ragnar turned slowly and looked up at the fox.

"Who wants to know?" he asked insolently.

"I'm Flick, the Warden of Watersmeet. Call your animals to order."

"And if I don't?" Ragnar asked.

"Then you'll have to leave the village."

Ragnar laughed, but Gorm leapt to his hindpaws and pulled out his sword. It was Sandor's sword that Gorm had taken from Vair, and Vair felt all his grief reawaken at the sight of it. He had still done nothing to avenge Sandor, and as his wound gradually weakened him, he felt all hope slipping away.

"No!" Kyria said as the ferret swung the sword at Flick.

Flick wasn't armed, but Gorm's threat didn't seem to worry him. He stepped aside and brought his paw down on the ferret's wrist with a swift chopping motion. The ferret let out a curse and dropped the sword. He stood rubbing his wrist and fixed Flick with a murderous glare.

"Can't you keep your band under control?" Flick asked furiously.

"Don't get excited," Ragnar drawled. "They're only having fun."

"It's not my idea of fun," Flick said.

Flora came to join him and snatched up Gorm's sword just as he was bending down to retrieve it.

"Hey, that's mine!" Gorm said.

Flora bared her teeth. "Will ye be fighting me for it then, laddie?"

The ferret snarled, and his paw went to the wickedly long dagger in his belt, but he made no other move. Vair guessed that better beasts than him had thought twice before attacking Flora. He couldn't help enjoying Gorm's anger and feeling relief that the evil ferret no longer carried Sandor's sword.

Ragnar stretched lazily and got to his hindpaws to face Flick; his crew of bandits gathered around him. Gorm slunk over to his side, still uneasily watching Flora, who shadowed him with a mean look in her eye and a firm grip on the sword.

"Look, we don't want any trouble," said Flick. "The Watersmeet Fair is supposed to be a happy time."

"That's all right, then," said Ragnar. "We're all happy, aren't we, lads?"

"Aye, Cap'n," the band replied, grinning.

"Then keep yourselves to yourselves, and don't annoy the other animals," said Flick.

Ragnar laughed in his face. "Make us," he challenged. "If you can."

"Very well," Flick said. "According to our law—"

The silver fox laughed again, interrupting what Flick was saying. He spat to one side. "That's for your law," he said. "I'm talking about a fight. But you wouldn't dare fight us, would you? All by yourself?"

"He's not all by himself," said Flora immediately. "I'm with ye, Flick."

"And me." Two of the otters had disappeared, but the third stepped forward and touched his paw to his nautical cap. "Captain Taffrail of the *River Queen*, at your service."

"And me," Kyria added.

Vair felt suddenly hopeful, but even while Flick and his friends were speaking, he realized that there were still only four of them to fight against seven tough, battle-scarred bandits. Flora looked as if she was a formidable warrior, but Vair couldn't be sure about the others. His hope died. No one here was strong enough to defeat Ragnar's gang.

Flick shook his head. "Thank you all, but no. I will not have bloodshed so close to the Fair. Not if I can avoid it."

He looked Ragnar thoughtfully up and down. The silver fox gave Flick a mocking bow and started to swagger toward the inn door.

Flick called him back. "Captain Ragnar! Where are you going?"

"To find ourselves rooms, Warden. All this arguing has made us tired, hasn't it, lads?"

The rest of the crew agreed noisily.

"Then see you behave yourselves," said Flick. "If there's any trouble, I'll know the cause."

"I'm terrified," said Ragnar. "Come on, lads."

"Here, what about my sword?" the ferret complained.

"You can collect it from me when the Fair is over," said Flick. "Just before you leave."

"Leave?" said Ragnar. "Who said anything about leaving? We like it here, don't we, lads?"

"Aye, Cap'n," his band chorused again.

Vair saw Kyria exchange a worried glance with Shadow. Clearly they had never imagined that Ragnar and his crew meant to settle in the village.

"No one has invited you to stay," said Flick steadily.

"You sayin' we're not welcome?" the ferret asked aggressively.

"All animals of *good will* are welcome," said Flick. "Animals who want to settle down and work with us and take part in village life. Not those who want to make trouble."

"Now, listen here, Warden." Captain Ragnar stepped forward, fastened his paw into Flick's neckerchief and drew Flick toward him so they faced each other, nose to nose. "If we say we're going to stay, we'll stay. And you'll do what we tell you because there's none of you got the guts to do anything else."

"No guts?" roared Flora. She raised the sword she had taken from Gorm. "No guts? Ye'll not say that twice to a MacStripe!"

"No, Flora," Flick said. "Not now."

At the same moment, Gorm said, "Get lost, pussycat."

"Pussycat!" Flora drew her lips back so that her fangs snarled at Gorm. Her striped tail bristled out to twice its size. "D'ye know the motto o' the MacStripes? 'Touch not the cat without a glove.' I'll make ye sorry ye called me pussycat!"

"We can't wait," drawled Ragnar. He turned back to Flick, still holding his neck cloth bunched up in his paw. "You lot—you're living here so nice and soft and cozy. You've got everything you want, and life is easy. But you don't know what to do to keep it. You haven't the guts, and you haven't the strength."

Vair saw Kyria and the squirrel exchange another despairing glance, as though they thought, *It's true!* They were gripping each other's paws hard.

"So we're just going to do as we like," said Ragnar. "And you can't do anything to stop us. And pretty soon there'll be other villages in this nice, soft country that'll have to learn what you're learning now."

Vair remembered the gathering of bandits in the hills, and he shivered to think of them robbing and killing their way through this peaceful, happy country. He wanted to tell Flick what he had seen, but he didn't suppose that Flick would want to listen or would believe anything he said.

"What do you mean?" Flick asked sharply. "What other villages?"

"Never you mind." Ragnar released him and pushed him away. "You'll find out, soon enough."

"Let me cut him," Flora pleaded. "Let me cut him into wee, small bits!"

Ragnar ignored her. "So we'll just go and find rooms here at the inn," he said. "What's it called? The Merry Ferret? That'll do us nicely. You're merry, aren't you, Gorm?"

"Oh, aye, Cap'n," the huge ferret said as he danced a jig around Flick. "I'm merry as anything, I am. Har, har."

The rest of the band broke into cackling laughter as Captain Ragnar bowed once again to Flick and led them into the inn. Vair hesitated, wishing there was something he could say.

"Here, you, scum!" Ragnar yelled at Vair. "Get a move on!"

Vair glanced at him and then at Flick and his friends, who were bunched together, watching Ragnar and murmuring among themselves. None of them were paying any attention to Vair.

Vair got up, hefted his bundle, and followed Ragnar inside.

Trouble

Early the next morning, Kyria walked up to the Fair Field just north of the village, where visiting traders had already begun pitching their tents under the trees around the edge and setting up wooden stands to display their wares.

Kyria lifted her skirts and the white tip of her tail clear of the morning dew. The grass was heavy with it, but the sun had begun to draw up the ground mist, promising a hot day. Blackbirds were singing cheerfully in the bushes.

"Good morning, Mistress Floss," Kyria greeted a rabbit weaver from Flaxhall, who was a regular visitor to the Fair. "Did you have a good journey?"

Floss paused in uncording a bale of linen pieces. "Fair to middlin', thank you, Miss Kyria. But my Bodo, he's picked up a thorn or something. He can barely put his hindpaw to the ground."

"Send him down to see me, and I'll have a look at it," Kyria promised, even though she suspected that Bodo had invented his "thorn" so that he could sit in the Merry Ferret while his mother did all the work.

"And there were a couple of rats just now," Floss went on, "poking and prying through my goods, even though I told them the fair hasn't started yet. Do you know who they are, Miss Kyria?"

"I think I do," Kyria said, beginning to worry about what Ragnar's crew were up to. "I'm sorry they bothered you, Mistress Floss. I'll have a word with Flick."

A little further on, she heard a cheerful whistling and saw some squirrels from Acornbury beginning to unpack the musical instruments they crafted in the oak woods to the north. Kyria was relieved to see that no one was making trouble for them. She waved and called to them that she would tell Shadow they had arrived.

As she was turning toward home, she heard a cry of indignation. She looked around just in time to see one of Ragnar's rats push a mole trader into the long grass and brambles at the edge of the field.

"Hey, stop that!" she called.

As she hurried over, a second rat appeared out of the mole's tent, stuffing a crusty bread roll into his mouth.

"Nah, it ain't here," he mumbled with his mouth full.

What's not here? Kyria asked herself. *What are they looking for?*

"Here now, that's my breakfast!" the mole protested, struggling out of the brambles and sucking a scratched forepaw.

"I said stop that!" Kyria repeated.

The first rat looked her up and down, sneering. "Make us."

He had been rooting through a wicker hamper filled with pots packed in straw, and now he stood up, tossing one of them from paw to paw.

"Do you want to buy that?" asked the mole.

"Nah, it's rubbish," the rat said.

He threw the pot over to the other rat, who made no attempt to catch it. The pot crashed to the ground and smashed. "Oh, clumsy me, I missed it," said the rat, and snickered.

Kyria whipped out her belt knife. Darting swiftly at the nearest rat, she twisted his forepaw behind his back and held the knife point close to his twitching snout. "I think you should say sorry," she suggested.

"Run her through!" the rat squealed to his mate.

But the mole had ducked inside his tent and came out again, gripping a stout club. He waved it at the other rat. "Keep your paws off her!" he said.

"Well?" Kyria said.

"Sorry," her prisoner muttered.

Kyria let him go and pushed him away. "Now take yourselves out of here."

The two rats retreated, looking threateningly over their shoulders. "You wait 'til Cap'n Ragnar hears about this!" one of them whined.

Kyria stood with her knife at the ready until they were well away. "I'm sorry about that," she said to the mole.

The mole mopped his brow. "Wasn't your fault, miss."

"I'll tell Wiggin to send you up some breakfast from the Merry Ferret," Kyria promised.

The mole brightened up and was whistling softly as he picked up the pieces of broken pot. Kyria said good-bye and was on her way to the inn when she heard a sudden rush of wings. She looked up; darkness blotted out the sun. A peregrine falcon plummeted from the sky on slate-blue wings and landed with his talons and raking beak only inches away from her.

"Sir Peregrine!" she exclaimed. "I wish you wouldn't do that."

The falcon's yellow eyes glared. "What is going on here?" he demanded. "What do these rats want?"

Kyria let out a long sigh. "Oh, you saw that, did you? I wish I knew. They seem to be searching for something, but I don't know what."

The peregrine falcon made a snapping noise with his beak. "And what do you intend to do about it? If they're not stopped, the fair will be ruined."

"I'm going to tell Flick," Kyria said patiently.

"And what will he do?"

"I don't know." Kyria tried not to be dismayed by the falcon's furious expression and sharp talons. She knew he was a decent bird in spite of his fierce ways, but he could be very difficult to deal with. "Sir Peregrine, you're welcome to Watersmeet, but you're not in charge here. If you want to help, then—"

"Once the falcons were stewards of the kingdom, under the royal eagles," Sir Peregrine informed her haughtily. "We were in charge everywhere."

"That was a long time ago," said Kyria.

"Harrumph!" His eyes blazing, Sir Peregrine stared at her for a moment more, and then, with a few strong wing beats, he took to the sky again.

Kyria watched him go. First the rats, making trouble, and now Sir Peregrine with his complaints . . . the bright morning was spoiled. She couldn't help thinking that the whole of the fair would be spoiled as well unless they could get rid of Ragnar and his gang.

Shadow had gone out early into the fields to find somewhere quiet to practice his flute solo for the Fair Feast. It was almost midday before he was satisfied and set off back to the village.

Just before he reached the meeting point of the Broad River and the Spine, Shadow saw three figures coming down the path toward him. He recognized Gorm, the huge ferret who seemed to be Ragnar's lieutenant, and his two stoats. The stoats had their swords out, slashing at the clumps of grass and wildflowers that grew along the riverbank.

Shadow glanced over his shoulder; no one else was in sight. There was nowhere he could hide, and if he tried to run away, they would catch him. *Maybe they aren't looking for trouble*, he told himself. *I haven't anything they want.*

As he drew level with them, he stepped off the path, giving them plenty of room to pass. He said, "Good morning," and tried to look as if he meant it.

One of the stoats lurched to one side and bumped into him as they went past, almost knocking Shadow off his hindpaws. As Shadow regained his balance, the stoat grabbed him by the shirt collar.

"Clumsy oaf," the stoat said. "You nearly sent me flyin'."

"But I—" Shadow broke off. Three sets of eyes were watching him intently. Three sets of teeth grinned at him. *So that's the game*, he thought. "Sorry," he said.

Gorm the ferret grabbed Shadow's ear and twisted it painfully. He bent over Shadow so that the squirrel could look straight at his uneven teeth and smell his foul breath. "Sorry *what?*"

Shadow knew what answer he wanted, and he had no ambition to be a hero. "Sorry, sir," he said.

The stoat pushed him away roughly, but Gorm still kept the grip on his ear.

"I reckon you need teachin' a few manners," he said. "What d'you say, lads?"

The stoats chorused agreement, their eyes bright and wickedly amused. Gorm shook Shadow by the ear, almost lifting him off his hindpaws. Tears of pain sprang to Shadow's eyes; he hoped the ferret wouldn't think he was going to cry.

"What's yer name, tree-rat?" Gorm asked.

"Shadow, sir."

The second stoat had drawn closer to him, stroking his tail and pretending to admire it. Shadow shivered.

"Fine tail," said the stoat. "Keeps the flies off, does it?"

"Er . . . yes."

"Suppose I cut it off," the stoat said, squinting along his sword blade. "Then it could keep flies off of me."

Shadow wasn't sure if he really meant it or if they were just trying to scare him.

"And what've you got there?" Gorm asked. "Bit of firewood?"

Suddenly Shadow felt cold and sick, and really frightened for the first time. "It's my flute, sir. I'm a musician."

"And are you goin' to give us a nice tune?"

"If—if you want."

"Nah. I hates music. Get it, Ketch."

"No!" As one of the stoats lunged forward and grabbed the flute, Shadow started struggling furiously. He tried to kick out at Gorm to free himself; the huge ferret howled as Shadow's hindpaw found its mark.

Then sharp pain lanced through Shadow's paw as the stoat twisted it, and his grip on the flute relaxed. The stoat caught it as it fell and held it up, dancing backwards in triumph.

"Stop it!" Shadow cried. "Give it back!"

Instead, the stoat tossed the flute into the river, where it bobbed on the current and started to float downstream. Gorm thrust Shadow forward sharply so that he fell to his forepaws on the path.

"You want it, you go an' fetch it," he said.

Shadow stared up at him wildly, and then at the flute. The current was strong here, just below the meeting of the rivers, and it was bearing the flute swiftly away. If it was carried down into the lake, he would never see it again.

Desperately he pulled off his shoes and shirt, and dove into the river.

As he came up, he heard raucous laughter from the bank. Ignoring it, he managed to locate the flute, reached out for it, and grasped it.

When he turned to swim back to the bank, he saw that they were waiting for him.

They let him get a grip on the overhanging grasses and begin to haul himself out. Then Gorm put one booted hindpaw on his chest.

"No—don't!" Shadow gasped.

Gorm only laughed and thrust hard at him.

The clump of grass tore away, and Shadow fell back into the water. When he resurfaced the current had carried him farther out into the river. The ferret and the two stoats were pacing him along the bank. There was still no one else in sight.

Shadow swam for the bank again, grimly determined. It was harder to make headway when he was holding on to the flute, but he would not let it go.

This time, as he grasped for a stone that jutted out of the bank, one of the stoats brought his boot heel down hard on his paw.

Shadow fell back again, treading water as the current swept him on. The bank was steeper here, and he couldn't see anywhere else he could climb out. The river was growing wider as it approached the lake, and he knew he was too tired now to swim across to the other side.

He tried to call for help, and swallowed a mouthful of water.

Even though the sun was shining, he began to feel cold. His fur was soaked; his tail felt heavy, dragging him down. Choking and gasping for breath, he grabbed at a trailing spray of leaves, and missed. The last thing he heard as his head went under was loud laughter from the riverbank.

New Friends

Vair crossed the bridge over the Spine and started to walk down the path towards the lake. Ragnar had sent him to find Gorm and the two stoats, Ketch and Snarg, so they could organize a thorough search for the silver horn the Lord Owl had asked for.

The sun was shining, and the fields beside the path were fresh and green. As he left the village behind him, Vair wondered what would happen if he just went on walking, away from Ragnar and the rest of them. If he could escape, he could look for his mother and the young ones.

But his wound was throbbing worse than ever, and he guessed that if he tried to escape, he would not get far. And if he left Ragnar, he would lose his best chance at revenge for Sandor's death.

Then he saw Gorm and the stoats. They were standing on the path, laughing and looking at something in the water. Vair noticed the swimmer and recognized Shadow, the young red squirrel who had been outside the Merry Ferret the day before. He had scarcely realized that something was wrong when he saw the squirrel's head vanish under the water.

Blind anger swept over Vair. He covered the few yards that separated him from Ragnar's bullies without letting himself think. Gorm and the stoats did not see him coming.

The huge ferret let out a yell of surprise as Vair cannoned into him from behind and thrust him into the river. He went under, thrashing and howling.

Vair grabbed Ketch by the jacket collar and pulled him backwards. As he lost his balance the stoat let go of his sword; Vair snatched it up. He turned on the second stoat with teeth bared. For a few seconds, Snarg faced him.

"Come on," Vair said. "You were brave enough just now. You're not frightened of me, are you?"

"Frightened of you, scum?" Snarg laughed unconvincingly. "I'll eat you for breakfast!" He put his paw on his sword hilt, but as Vair stepped forward, he began to back off. "I can't be bothered with you," he said, and fled back toward the village.

Ketch was rolling around on the path, moaning that his back was broken. Vair jabbed him with the sword. "Get up! Or I'll break the rest of you to match."

The stoat stared wild-eyed at the blade that menaced him and scrambled, whimpering, along the path. He did not get to his hindpaws until he was well out of range. "Wait 'til the Cap'n hears about this," he whined as he staggered away after his companion.

Vair turned to the water's edge. He was wondering if Shadow had drowned after all and then saw him under the overhang of the bank. He had managed to clutch a projecting root, and he was clinging there with his eyes closed. He looked too exhausted to do

anything more.

Dropping the sword, Vair knelt and reached down until he could grasp Shadow's paws. In one of them he was clinging to a flute. Vair hauled him upwards.

"Come on," he said. "It's all right now."

Shadow's eyes flickered open and terror sprang into them. Vair felt that look like a sword blade. He turned his face aside and finished dragging the squirrel out of the river to the safety of the bank, where he huddled, shivering and coughing water.

Vair straightened up slowly. A short way downstream, he could see Gorm pulling himself up on to the bank, snarling and furious. There was no way of escaping him. Vair gripped the sword again and waited.

Gorm sauntered toward him, river water streaming down his face. Vair expected him to attack, but he did not draw his belt knife. To Vair's surprise, there was fear in his face, though he tried to hide it as he drew closer.

"Oh, no, scum," he said. "I'm not goin' to kill you. I'm goin' to leave you for Ragnar. He'll kill you slow and interestingly. I'll look forward to that, scum."

"You do that," Vair said.

He kept his eyes on Gorm as the ferret retreated, and did not lower his sword until he was out of sight. Then he looked around, saw Shadow's discarded shirt on the bank, and fetched it for him.

"Here. You'd better get back and change into something dry."

The squirrel sat up, took the shirt, and clumsily tried to dry himself off with it. He gave Vair a clear, considering look, not frightened any longer.

"Why did you help me?" he asked. "You're one of them."

"No, I'm—" Vair began to protest, and then shrugged. "It doesn't matter." He held out a paw. "I'll walk back with you, in case they're still hanging about."

As he took Shadow's paw and helped him to stand, a stab of pain from his wound shot through his shoulder. He couldn't help wincing.

"What's the matter?" Shadow asked. "Did they hurt you?"

"No, it's an old wound. It's nothing."

"You should let Kyria see it. She's our healer. I'll take you there."

He retrieved his shoes and began hurrying back along the path. Vair kept up with him in case there was trouble waiting for them up ahead, but Gorm and the stoats had disappeared.

When they reached the bridge, he said, "Your healer won't want to help me."

"Kyria's not like that," said Shadow. He was

shivering violently, but still looking at Vair with that bright-eyed gaze. "Besides . . ." he added with a touch of shyness, "you helped me."

He crossed the bridge and led the way along the path beside the bank of the Broad River. Vair followed almost as if he was in a dream. He knew that he could not expect help from any of the villagers, but there was something about Shadow that made him impossible to refuse.

At last the squirrel climbed the bank and knocked at a door set in it. It swung open, and Kyria looked out.

"Shadow!" she exclaimed, when she saw the state the squirrel was in. "What happened? And what have you brought *him* here for?" she added with a look of dislike at Vair.

Vair, feeling ashamed, started to back away. Shadow grabbed his paw.

"No—no, Kyria, you don't understand," he said. "He saved my life. And he's hurt."

"Oh, come in, the pair of you," Kyria said, dragging Shadow over the threshold and holding the door open for Vair to follow. "Shadow, when are you going to learn to stay out of trouble?"

The squirrel tried to laugh, but he was shaking too hard. "I don't—don't know, Kyria."

"I do. When the eagles return, that's when. In other words, never." She pushed him toward an inner door.

"You know where the towels are. Leave your wet clothes there; I'll dry them later." When he had disappeared, she turned back to Vair. "Now you."

Vair looked around. He stood in a large kitchen, with a stone-flagged floor. Sun shone in through a window cut in the bank. The walls were lined with shelves of earthenware pots and jars. Bundles of herbs hung from the beams, and a kettle hissed gently on the kitchen stove. The chairs by the fire and the couch under the window were heaped with bright patchwork cushions. Vair was relieved to see that Flick was not there.

"Well?" said Kyria. "What happened?"

Vair explained to her as much as he knew. By the time he had finished, Shadow was back, his drying fur sticking up in tufts and a quilt wrapped around him.

"Come and sit by the fire," Kyria said. "If you catch cold, there'll be no music for the Fair Feast." She pushed him into one of the chairs beside the stove.

"Kyria," Shadow said, "he's hurt, and—" He broke off. "I don't know your name."

"It's Vair," he said, looking at the floor.

"Vair," Kyria repeated. She smiled at him, and Vair suddenly felt that perhaps she and Shadow would be his friends after all. She gestured toward the couch under the window. "Come and sit over here and show me where you're hurt."

Vair sat down in the full sunlight and pulled back his shirt to show the wound. Though it had closed up, it was swollen and felt hot, and pain throbbed through it.

Kyria examined it carefully, letting out a long whistle through her teeth. "Where did you get that?" she asked.

"Gorm did it," said Vair.

"Gorm?" Kyria asked with arched eyebrows. "That big useless ferret? You fight among yourselves, then?"

"I wasn't with them then!" Vair said indignantly. "I wouldn't—"

"You're not one of them," Shadow said. "I know you're not."

Kyria looked at Vair, rubbing her muzzle thoughtfully. "I think you'd better tell us."

Vair began the story of how Ragnar and his band had attacked Vair's family on their way downriver. Vair described the fight, and then how he had awakened later to discover that his father was dead and his mother and the younger children nowhere to be found.

His voice started to shake. Vair clenched his paws and stared at the floor as he forced himself to go on to the end. When he had finished, he buried his face in his paws and shed all the tears for his father and mother and the young ones that he had kept trapped inside himself until now.

After a moment, he felt a touch on his arm. He looked up to see Shadow at his side.

"Oh, I'm so sorry," the squirrel whispered. He tried to smile. "But you're not alone anymore. You have friends here. We'll help you look for your family."

Vair rubbed his paws over his face. Kyria had fetched two mugs and was measuring some kind of syrup into them from a pottery flask. "This is valerian and honey," she said. "Drink it. You'll feel better." She topped up the mugs with hot water from the kettle and handed one to Vair and one to Shadow.

Vair clasped his paws gratefully around the mug and sipped the hot liquid. It relaxed his throat and spread a soothing warmth all through his body.

"Listen," said Kyria. "That wound of yours is infected. I shall have to open it up again and clean it. It's going to hurt, but it's the only way. All right?"

Vair set his teeth. "All right."

"Finish your drink while I get ready."

While Vair swallowed the last of the hot cordial, Kyria spread a clean cloth over the cushions on the couch, assembled bandages and salve on the kitchen table, and poured hot water into a bowl. Then she came to stand over Vair, a thin, sharp knife in her paw.

"Lie down," she said. "It won't take long."

Vair lay back, and Shadow crouched beside him and

took both of Vair's paws into his own. Shadow was looking wide-eyed and anxious.

"Kyria, will he be all right?" Shadow asked.

"Of course, he will. Don't fuss," Kyria comforted.

Almost before Vair realized it, she bent over him, and her knife flashed. A cry was torn out of him as pain like a red-hot needle stabbed his shoulder. A greenish yellow pus started to ooze out of the gash Kyria had made; Vair heard a horrified gasp from Shadow.

His senses swam, and when his head cleared again, Kyria was bathing the wound. Her paws were quick and steady. Already Vair could feel a difference; it was still painful, but the heat and the swelling were gone.

"That's good, Vair," Kyria said. "A few more days and it would have been a lot nastier. Now . . ." She fetched a pot and smeared a thick, greenish salve into the wound. It had a sharp, clean smell. "Self-heal," she said. "There's nothing better."

Deftly she wound a bandage around Vair's chest and shoulder, and fastened it with a neat knot. "There. Done. You're to come every day and let me change that dressing."

"Thank you," said Vair. He was lying back on the cushions, limp now that the pain was ebbing. He almost felt he could sleep, but he made himself sit up.

"I'd better go. Ragnar might be looking for me."

"But you can't go back to him!" Shadow protested.

Vair shrugged. "I don't want to get you into trouble."

"Ragnar wants trouble in any case," said Kyria, looking disgusted at the thought of the silver fox. "I don't think anything you do will make it worse. He says he's going to settle down here, and he's looking for something—"

"Do you know what he wants?" Shadow asked Vair.

"Yes," Vair said softly.

Kyria was clearing up the equipment she had used for the operation, but she stopped what she was doing and turned eagerly to Vair. "Is there anything you can tell us—anything that would help?"

"I'll tell you what I know," said Vair.

He began the story of the bandit meeting and how the Lord Owl had said that he wanted to rule Riverbourne. Kyria and Shadow stared at him, wide-eyed with horror as they realized that Ragnar was only the beginning of the trouble they would have to face.

"Then," Vair finished, "when the other bandits left, the Lord Owl made Ragnar stay behind. He sent him here to look for a silver horn. I don't know why, but the Lord Owl wants it more than anything."

Shadow gasped. Kyria gave Vair a sharp look and

then crossed the kitchen and took something down from one of the shelves near the kitchen range. When she turned back, Vair saw that she was holding a silver drinking horn in a wooden stand.

"A horn like this one?" Kyria asked.

The Silver Horn

Vair leapt to his hindpaws. "Where did you get that?" he exclaimed.

"We've had it as long as I can remember," Kyria said. "My great-grandmother brought it back from her travels. It's my father's favorite cup."

Kyria held out the horn to him, and Vair turned it around in his forepaws. It felt heavy. Around the rim was a pattern of eagles' wings; the rest of the horn was covered with flowing marks engraved into the silver. Vair couldn't decide whether they were just decoration or whether they held a message that he could not read.

"This must be the horn the Lord Owl wants," he said. "I don't know why, but it can't be for anything good. He mustn't get it. Kyria, you'd better hide it."

As he spoke, the sound of footsteps and loud voices came from the path outside. Someone hammered on

the door. Kyria snatched the horn from Vair, threw up the lid of a chest at the far side of the kitchen, and put the horn inside.

"Lock the door," she said to Vair. She closed the lid of the chest and sat on it.

The hammering came again and Ragnar's voice yelling, "Open up!" Before Vair could reach the door, the silver fox thrust it open and strode into the kitchen, followed by Ketch the stoat and one of the rats.

"What do you want?" Kyria asked tartly.

Ragnar stood looking around him as if he owned the

place. Ketch grabbed the sword Vair had taken from him, which Vair had left propped up against the kitchen table, and glared at the pine marten as he stuck it back in its sheath.

"I said, what do you want?" Kyria repeated.

Instead of answering, Ragnar snapped out a command to Ketch and the rat, who started to search the kitchen shelves, poking behind the flasks and bowls, opening boxes and earthenware crocks. Ketch knocked over a whole row of jars; Shadow scrambled across the kitchen and managed to catch one of them, but the rest smashed, and the ointment inside oozed stickily over the flagstones. The rat took the lid off a pot of honey, dipped a paw into it, and started sucking greedily.

"You can't just walk in here—" Kyria began furiously.

"Oh, yes, we can," said Ragnar. "Who's to stop us? As for you—" He grabbed Vair by the neck fur and pulled him close. "Scum, you've made Gorm very unhappy. And when he's unhappy, he gets nasty. I wouldn't want to be you, little scum."

Vair pulled free. "I don't care. He doesn't frighten me."

Ragnar pulled his lips back in an ugly snarl. "Then you're even more stupid than I thought. Gorm's going to mash you to a pulp."

"He can try," said Vair.

Ragnar let out a short bark of laughter and turned back to Ketch and the rat. "Well? Anything?"

"No, Cap'n," said Ketch. He pointed to the inner door. "Shall I look in here?"

"What do you think, idiot? I told you to look every-where," Ragnar snapped.

Ketch and the rat disappeared through the door. Vair could hear them crashing around as they searched the other rooms. Kyria's white tail tip was flicking back and forth, as if she wanted to follow, but she didn't dare leave the chest she was sitting on.

Just then there were more footsteps on the path outside, and Flick stepped in through the open door. "What's going on?" he said.

"It's Ragnar and his fools," said Kyria. "They just walked in here. They're looking for something."

"Then they can just walk out again," Flick said calmly. "Captain Ragnar, I've told you before about making trouble. This is my house, and you're not welcome here."

Ragnar laughed. "I'll stay as long as I want. What are you going to do about it?"

Flick didn't answer the question in words. Instead, he went through the inner door and reappeared a moment later, pushing Ketch in front of him and dragging the rat by the scruff of the neck. The rat was wailing miserably.

"Out," said Flick, shoving both of them toward the outer door.

"Have you found it?" Ragnar asked.

Ketch shook his head. "We ain't finished looking, Cap'n."

Ragnar eyed Flick aggressively, but Vair guessed he was thinking twice before tangling with him. "Right," he said at last. "We'll go, but we'll be back. And you, scum," he added, jerking his head at Vair. "Get moving."

"He's not coming with you!" Shadow said. "We're his friends now."

Flick looked surprised until Kyria explained quickly what had happened. "We don't have slaves here," she finished, speaking angrily to Ragnar. "You can't make him go with you."

"Can't I?" the silver fox said.

His paw went to the hilt of his sword, but before he could draw the blade, Flick grabbed his wrist. "Just go quietly, and nobody will get hurt."

"Who's going to make me?" Ragnar sneered. "You? Don't make me laugh! I could beat you with one paw tied behind my back."

"You think so?" Flick said. He let Ragnar go. "How would you like to prove that?"

"What do you mean?" Ragnar asked suspiciously.

"I'm challenging you," Flick said. "Single combat. If you win, you can stay here and do what you want. If you lose, you go away and stop bothering us. What do you say?"

Ragnar hesitated. Vair thought that he looked uncertain. Although he was younger and bigger than Flick, he couldn't be sure of beating him. The old fox looked like a formidable animal.

"Well?" Flick said, when Ragnar didn't reply. "You can't be afraid of me, surely? I'll even let you use both paws."

"Go on, Cap'n," Ketch said eagerly. "You can make mincemeat of him."

"Shut up, fool," Ragnar said. "I don't have to fight him. We're staying, whether he likes it or not."

"I see," said Flick. "You like throwing your weight around, but you're scared to meet me in a fair fight."

"Here, Cap'n," said the rat. "You ain't goin' to let him talk like that, are you?"

Ragnar glanced uneasily at his followers. Vair thought that Flick was right; the silver fox was afraid to fight, but if he refused he would lose the respect of the rest of his crew. If he backed down now, he would have to slink away, defeated.

"How do I know you'll fight fair?" Ragnar blustered.

"I could say the same," Flick retorted. "I think we'll just have to trust each other."

Flick was grinning faintly, as if he could see that he had worried Ragnar.

"Go on, Cap'n," Ketch said. "Slice his ears off!"

Ragnar drew himself up and tugged at his grubby scarlet coat. "All right," he said. "Captain Ragnar isn't afraid to fight anybody. But you challenged me," he added. "It's my choice of time and place."

Flick nodded. "Choose, then."

"Well . . ." Vair thought he could see a crafty glint in Ragnar's eyes. "How about tomorrow morning, first thing? And on the village green. Then everybody can see it's a fair fight."

"So they can," Flick agreed. "Very well, then. Tomorrow morning it is."

The Prophecy

The sun was going down when Vair peered cautiously out of Kyria's door. "All clear," he said.

He climbed down the bank to the path beside the river. Flick had lent him a cloak, and the silver horn was bundled up underneath it. He beckoned to Shadow to join him, and together they hurried upriver, away from the center of the village.

When Ragnar and the others had left Flick's house, Kyria and Shadow had cleared up the mess in the kitchen, while Vair told Flick what was happening.

Flick sat in the chair beside the kitchen range and turned the silver horn over and over in his paws. "My grandmother brought this back from her travels," he said, when Vair had finished his story. "Kyria, you were only a cub when she died. Do you remember her?"

"Oh, yes!" Kyria paused in sweeping up the broken

jars. "She sat in that chair where you are now and told wonderful stories."

"Granny was a great traveler when she was young," Flick went on. "She said she had a fight with pirates and brought this back from their hoard. No telling where *they* got it. My father put a stopper in it to block the end and made the wooden stand so he could use it as a drinking horn."

"And now the Lord Owl is looking for it," said Vair.

"And what for?" Kyria asked. "What good is it to him? That's what I want to know."

"He wants to rule Riverbourne," said Vair. "But I can't see how the horn will help him to do that."

"Isn't there anything we can do to stop him?" Shadow asked despairingly.

"We must warn everyone in all the other villages," Flick said. "I'll see if I can get Sir Peregrine to organize some of the birds."

"That should please him—he *loves* organizing," said Kyria, hiding a grin as she swept vigorously.

"And they can keep a lookout for your family at the same time, Vair," said Flick.

Vair smiled gratefully at him. For the first time, he began to hope that before long he would be reunited with his mother and his brother and sister again.

Kyria began to set bowls and plates on the table for a meal. "And what are we going to do with the horn? We have to find a safe place for it."

"Ragnar won't dare come back here," said Vair.

"He might," said Kyria. "He was interrupted. Shadow, I think you should look after it."

"Me?" said the squirrel, alarmed.

"You're right at the top of that huge oak tree. I don't suppose Ragnar and his crew will do much climbing— even the stoats. And if you pull your ladder up, they won't be able to see that anyone lives there."

Reluctantly, Shadow agreed. Now he led Vair up the Broad River until they came to an oak tree growing out of the bank, with its branches stretching out over the water. A rope ladder dangled down close to the trunk, but there was no other sign that the tree was inhabited.

Ignoring the ladder, Shadow sprang up the trunk and disappeared among the leaves. More slowly, encumbered by the horn and the cloak, Vair followed him until he came to a platform of planks nailed across a couple of stout branches. The platform was railed with twigs woven into a lattice.

Shadow was looking over the rail. "Here we are," he said, and added shyly, "Welcome."

Vair climbed onto the platform. A door with a window above it led into the trunk of the tree. The platform was the veranda of Shadow's tree home. All around the oak leaves formed a green curtain, rustling gently in the breeze. Sunlight, reddening as evening approached, angled down through gaps in the foliage above.

Vair relaxed and brought the horn out from under his cloak. "Kyria was right," he said to Shadow, who was busily pulling up the rope ladder. "Ragnar will never find it up here."

Vair examined the horn again, admiring the flash of

sunlight on the silver and wondering what its secret might be.

"Those marks look almost like words," Vair said. "But if they are, I don't know how to read them."

"Let me see." Shadow took the horn and examined it. "Some old language, maybe," he suggested. "The horn must be old. I'm sure no one crafts anything like it these days."

He pulled out the stopper and, without warning, raised the horn to his lips to blow it.

"Shadow!" Vair exclaimed.

He grabbed for the horn, but Shadow had already lowered it, looking puzzled. "I can't get a note out of it."

"It's just as well," said Vair. "Shadow, was that really a good idea, when we're trying to *hide* the horn?"

"Oh . . ." Briefly the squirrel looked ashamed of himself. "I'm sorry. But it's really strange," he went on, squinting down the mouthpiece. "I should be able to sound it, but I can't."

"That's the least of our worries," said Vair. "If we—"

He broke off at a tearing sound of leaves and twigs from above. Looking up, he saw a peregrine falcon dropping like a stone through the branches. The falcon came to rest with the top of the veranda railing gripped in his powerful talons.

Shadow, with a gasp of alarm, had sprung backwards against the tree trunk, dropping the horn. Vair grabbed it and prepared to fight for it, only to relax a moment later as Shadow said, "Sir Peregrine, it's you! You scared me stiff!"

Apologizing didn't seem to occur to the fierce bird. He said, "That horn. Show it to me."

Vair glanced at Shadow, and when the squirrel nodded, he took the horn to Sir Peregrine. The falcon seized it in one talon and focused his piercing eyes on it. "I wonder . . ." He inspected it closely. "Yes!" he hissed softly. "It is!"

He half spread his wings, and for a second Vair thought that he was going to fly off with the horn. Then he settled again.

Fiercely he said, "Where did you get it? Where did you steal it from?"

"Steal it?" Shadow said nervously.

Vair stepped forward. "Now listen—"

Sir Peregrine glared at him. "Who are you, that I should listen to you?"

"His name is Vair," Shadow said. "Vair, this is Sir Peregrine."

Vair bowed. "It's an honor to meet you, sir."

His politeness did not seem to impress the arrogant falcon. His beak snapped irritably. "This horn," he said, "is the lost—the legendary—Horn of Eaglesmount."

Vair exchanged a glance with Shadow, but the squirrel was looking just as mystified as Vair himself felt. "I don't understand," he said. "What's the Horn of Eaglesmount?"

"Ignorant peasant!" said the falcon.

Vair set his teeth and managed to keep his temper. Sir Peregrine knew something vital; they couldn't afford to quarrel with him. "Tell us about it," he suggested.

Shadow sat down on the veranda and rested his chin on his paws. "Please do," he said. "I know Eaglesmount is where the High King of the Eagles used to live—in the days when there was a High King. But I don't know anything about the horn."

For a moment Sir Peregrine hesitated, still clutching the horn and glaring around with furious yellow eyes. Then he seemed to relax a little. "You have heard about the last battle of the last High King of the Eagles?" he asked.

Vair sat on the veranda beside Shadow. "I've heard of it," Vair said. "But it's only a legend, isn't it?"

"It is not a legend!" Sir Peregrine snapped. "It is true history. The last High King of the Eagles led his warriors to fight a black dragon that was ravaging this land. He defeated it, but he and all his warriors were destroyed.

"Before he flew to war, he made a prophecy about the one who would come after him. A badgersmith of great skill crafted a silver horn, and so powerfully did he make it that it could only be sounded by the rightful heir of the eagles."

"That's why I couldn't get a note out of it!" said Shadow.

Sir Peregrine went on. "The words of the prophecy were engraved on the horn so that they would never be forgotten. But after the last battle, when the ruling eagles were all dead, a time of chaos followed, and somehow the horn itself was lost. It has never been found again from that day to this—until now." He raised his talons with the horn gripped in them. "This is the Horn of Eaglesmount."

His voice shook on the last few words, and Vair realized wonderingly that the fierce bird was close to weeping.

"Just a minute," said Shadow. "I don't understand. Eagles—birds—can't blow horns. Their beaks get in the way."

"This is true," Sir Peregrine admitted. "It must be that the true heir to the royal eagles will not be an eagle."

"And not an owl, either," Shadow said thoughtfully.

"Who will it be, then?" Vair asked. "What does the prophecy say? Can you read it?"

Sir Peregrine gave him a disdainful look. "Naturally I can read it. The peregrine falcons were stewards to the royal eagles, and now we—only *we*—remember the days of their greatness and all their lore."

Vair wondered if that was true. The Lord Owl certainly knew about the horn. He knew enough to send Ragnar to Watersmeet to look for it. What Sir Peregrine had just told them explained why he was so determined to find it. If he meant to claim kingship over the whole of Riverbourne, it would help him enormously to have the Horn of Eaglesmount in his possession—and to keep it from the rightful heir. Perhaps the Lord Owl had a falcon in his service, or perhaps he had other ways of finding out what he needed to know.

"Sir Peregrine," Shadow said eagerly, "please read the prophecy to us."

The peregrine falcon raised the horn and spoke.

"You are alone and not alone,
Born to ascend the eagles' throne.
Your sign you draw from waters deep
While still your crown the waters keep.
The head of stone your voice will hear
And speak its secrets to your ear.
Dark is the doom of double blade,
Yet light springs in the forest shade.
Your fate awaits; your courage take
When darkness splits the frozen lake.
You are the one alone and not alone.
Rise, sound the horn, ascend the eagles' throne!"

"But what does it *mean?*" asked Shadow. He was looking puzzled, and then he suddenly brightened. "Vair! Listen— 'You are alone and not alone.' That could be you. You were alone when you came here, even though you were with Ragnar and his crew. And now you're not alone because we're your friends. You could be the heir to the eagles!"

Vair laughed out loud. "And what about the rest of the verse?"

"Well . . ." Shadow waved a paw, dismissing the problem. His eyes were shining. "Try to sound the horn, Vair. Please!"

Vair shrugged and took the horn from Sir Peregrine. Putting it to his lips, he blew hard, but not even the faintest squeak came out of it. "Satisfied?" he asked Shadow. "Cheer up," he added, as the squirrel looked disappointed. "At least we know now why the horn is important. We *must* keep it from Ragnar. The Lord Owl must *not* get it."

"What's this?" Sir Peregrine asked sharply.

Vair and Shadow between them told the story once again.

"Hah!" the falcon said. "Owls? Ruling here? Over my dead body!" He drew himself up and spread his wings. "I will speak with Flick."

He took off, rising through the branches, and vanished.

Shadow turned to open his door. "We must find a safe place to—" He broke off, clutching at Vair.

"What was that?"

They stood still, listening. Through the trees, in the gathering twilight, there came the hooting of an owl.

Treachery

Light was beginning to creep through her bedroom window as Kyria awoke. She sat up, not sure why she felt uneasy, until she remembered that this was the day her father was to fight with Ragnar.

When she had washed and dressed, she stoked the fire in the kitchen range and set a kettle of water to boil for chamomile tea. She scooped oatmeal from an earthenware crock and made dough for oatcakes, and when they were baking, she went to wake Flick.

Her father's room was empty, and his bed had not been slept in.

After her initial surprise, Kyria was annoyed. As animals gathered for the fair, Flick would often patrol the village by night to make sure there was no trouble. But she thought it was unwise of him to go out the night before the combat, when he would need to be well-rested.

"I'd better go and find him," she said to herself as she pulled the oatcakes from the oven, tossing her apron aside and taking a hooded cloak down from its peg on the back of the kitchen door. "Ragnar will only make more trouble if he isn't there on time."

She hurried along the path as far as the landing stage and the steps in the bank. A chilly mist hovered over the water, but ahead of her the sun was rising. The only sound was the lap of water over the stones of the riverbed.

Then, as Kyria climbed the steps, she began to hear singing—not Shadow's choir this time, but a raucous noise from the windows of the Merry Ferret. As she hurried around the corner of the inn, she saw Flora MacStripe hunched over one of the tables and staring into a steaming pot of spiced ale with a scowl on her face.

"A body can't sleep, Kyria," she said, the tip of her tail twitching irritably back and forth. "That racket went on all night."

Kyria was surprised that Ragnar hadn't felt the need of a good night's sleep either, but she had no time to think about that.

"Flora," she said, "have you seen Flick?"

"Is he not at home?" Flora asked.

Kyria explained.

"He's not here," the wildcat said, "and I haven't seen him. But I'll help ye look, Kyria."

Together they followed the path down to the Spine and then back to the Fair Field, where the traders who had camped overnight were already up and about. One or two of them had seen Flick the previous evening, but none of them since then.

"Maybe you'd better go home again, Kyria," Flora suggested as they turned back toward the village green. "Flick might be there by now."

"Maybe," said Kyria. From being annoyed with her father, she was becoming more worried with every minute that passed. Flick wasn't irresponsible. He wouldn't deliberately disappear on the morning of a fight as important as this one—a fight that could decide the whole future of the village. "If he doesn't come soon," she said, "Ragnar will call him a coward. Flora, I think something has happened to him."

Reaching the village green, they saw that Ragnar and his crew had appeared outside the inn. The scarlet-coated fox was lounging at one of the tables, and he hailed Kyria when he saw her.

"Where's your father? Skulking at home? Better fetch him, or he'll be late," Captian Ragner taunted.

Kyria didn't bother to reply. Hurrying past the

109

inn, she met Vair and Shadow coming up from the riverside. After a good night's rest, Vair looked bright and alert. Kyria could see what a strong, fit animal he had been before Gorm had wounded him.

"Kyria!" Shadow said, bounding up to her, his tail waving like a flag. "We found out something! Sir Peregrine—"

"Have you seen Flick?" Kyria interrupted. Whatever Shadow was excited about would have to wait.

Vair shook his head. "We knocked at your door, but there was no answer. Isn't he with you?"

"I don't know where he is," Kyria said, her paws gripped together anxiously.

"Have you tried down by the lake?" Shadow asked. "He might have gone to visit Captain Taffrail on the *River Queen*." When Kyria shook her head, he added, "Come on, Vair, we'll go and see."

Kyria watched them go. Flora clapped a heavy paw on her shoulder and said, "Let's try the woods by the Spine. Folk come in that way with carts. He might have gone to help."

The young vixen followed her friend back across the village green, ignoring the whistles and jeering from Ragnar and his crew as they passed the Merry Ferret.

By now the sun was up, and the clouds were clearing away. The woods were still and quiet. Dew sparkled on the grass and beaded on cobwebs in the undergrowth. Branches of honeysuckle arched over the rutted track.

When Kyria called to her father, there was no reply. Leaving the path, she pushed through clumps of bracken and around brambles, alert for any sign that her father had been that way. Flora began to do the same on the other side of the path.

Then Kyria skirted a hazel thicket and stopped short. In the long grass under the trees beyond, she saw a splash of russet fur and a fold of blue fabric that she recognized as her father's coat. She pressed her paws over her mouth, swallowed, and took a deep breath. "Flora! Flora, come here!"

As the wildcat crashed toward her through the undergrowth, she went forward. Flick was lying face down in the grass. He was quite still. A long-handled knife was sticking out of his back.

"Flick isn't dead," Kyria said steadily, "but he's badly hurt. He isn't fit to fight."

Flora called some of the villagers to carry Flick back to his house, where Kyria bandaged his wound. He was still unconscious, but breathing quietly, and Kyria thought it was safe to leave him with Mistress Wiggin to keep an eye on him, while she came to deal with Ragnar.

A crowd of worried villagers had gathered in front of the Merry Ferret. Vair and Shadow were among them, having returned from the *River Queen* with Captain Taffrail. Kyria told them what she could about her father's injuries.

"And will he recover?" asked Dunstan, the badger who was the village Elder.

"I think so," said Kyria. "And it's no thanks to you!" she added, whirling to face Ragnar, who was still lounging at his table, wearing a faint grin. "You had something to do with this!"

Ragnar yawned. When he spoke he sounded bored. "I never left the inn all night. Ask Wiggle there."

"It's true, Miss Kyria." Wiggin was hot and bothered. "They've been up all night, drinking and singing and carrying on, upsetting my other guests. Ragnar didn't hurt your dad. I'd have to swear to it."

"But he knows something," said Vair. "Or why did he stay up drinking, instead of going to bed? Unless he knew that he wouldn't have to fight this morning."

"You keep out of this, scum," said Ragnar.

"Vair's right!" Kyria didn't try to hide her anger. She was sick with worry about her father, and her patience with the silver fox and his crew had run out. Moreover, she had suddenly remembered where she had seen the long-handled knife that had been driven into Flick's back—stuck in the belt of Gorm the ferret. "Ask that stupid ferret where he was!"

Gorm just showed his uneven teeth in a grin.

"I can't say for certain," Wiggin said. "Ragnar was here all night, miss, but I'm not sure about all the others."

"There!" Kyria said to Dunstan. "Aren't you going to do something?"

Before the elderly badger could reply, Ragnar said, "Stop wasting my time. Flick challenged me to single combat, and he isn't here. That means I'm in charge of this village now. Go home, all of you."

The villagers muttered among themselves but stayed where they were.

Dunstan the Elder looked offended. "The villagers elect their Elder," he said. He tapped himself on the chest. "Me, as it happens. And if you—"

"Shut up, Grandad," said Ragnar. "I told you, I'm in charge now."

"Not without a fight," said Kyria hotly. "You've made sure that Flick can't fight you, but I can!"

"No, Kyria." Dunstan spoke with authority. "You're needed too much. Without your healing skills, what will happen to Flick?"

Kyria opened her mouth to protest, caught Dunstan's eye, and was silent.

While the badger was speaking, Flora MacStripe shouldered her way forward and stood glaring down at the silver fox. Her ears were laid close to her head and her tail lashed from side to side.

"On your hindpaws, fox," she said. "Do ye dare face the sword of a MacStripe?"

For a few seconds Kyria saw a look of sheer terror cross Ragnar's face. Then he pulled himself together. "Fight you, you overgrown kitten?" he sneered. "Why would I want to fight you? You're not a villager—this has got nothing to do with you."

Flora bared her fangs and snarled at him. "Ye yellow-livered coward!"

Gorm the ferret lifted his pot of ale as if he was going to throw it at Flora and then thought better of it. Downing the ale instead, he wiped his snout on the back of his paw and said, "Shove off, pussycat."

Flora's whiskers bristled in fury, but there was nothing she could do. Fuming, she retreated a pace or two.

Ragnar breathed on his claws and buffed them against his scarlet coat. "So that's settled. Unless there's any of you brave villagers want to challenge me instead?"

Despairingly, Kyria looked around her. Captain Taffrail was the only other animal who was capable of standing up to Ragnar, and like Flora, he was not a villager. The Watersmeet animals were not fighters. Already they were starting to move away, heads down, ashamed.

Then another voice spoke.

"Yes, I will," said Vair. "I challenge you, Ragnar."

The Challenge

Ragnar stared at Vair for a minute in stunned silence and then threw back his head and laughed. The rest of his crew broke into raucous cackles.

Vair stood waiting calmly, his back straight and his head erect. Inwardly his heart thumped with excitement, now that he had the chance to face up to Ragnar at last.

Under cover of the noise, Kyria murmured in his ear, "You're out of your mind!"

"No, I'm not," said Vair determinedly. "I can use a sword."

He felt Shadow seize his paw and looked down to see the squirrel gazing at him anxiously. "But can you beat Ragnar?"

"What about that wound?" Kyria asked. "You shouldn't fight until it's healed."

"It's much better now, thanks to you," said Vair. It

was true; he flexed his shoulder muscles and felt scarcely any pain.

"It could still slow you down," Kyria said worriedly.

"But then I haven't been up all night like Ragnar, swigging Barley Brew," said Vair. He smiled. "Don't worry, Kyria. Someone has to do this."

Kyria shook her head as if she was still not convinced, but all she said was, "You haven't even a sword."

"But I have!" Vair felt even more certain that what he was doing was right. "Do you remember the sword that Flick took from Gorm, the day we first arrived? That was my father's sword, and it's mine now. Do you know what Flick did with it?"

"It's in the chest in the kitchen," said Kyria. "Where I put the you-know-what."

"I'll fetch it," said Shadow. He streaked off around the corner of the inn.

Meanwhile Ragnar had recovered from his fit of laughter. Wiping his eyes with a grubby handkerchief, he said, "Oh, scum, you'll be the death of me. You can't challenge me, you stupid beast."

"Yes, I can," said Vair. "And I will be the death of you, Ragnar. I promise you that. You killed my father. My mother and the young ones fled from you, and now I don't know where they are. I'll take my revenge on you and save the village as well."

He heard a soft sound of applause and encouragement rising from the villagers, who had gathered around again. He straightened up, feeling a sudden pride. He would be their champion and perhaps be able to repay the help and friendship Kyria and Shadow had given him.

"Fine words," Ragnar sneered. "But I don't have to fight you, any more than I have to fight that mangy cat over there. You don't belong here."

"Yes, he does," said Kyria defiantly. "He's going to stay."

Dunstan the Elder stepped forward and stood in front of Vair. Vair looked up into the wise, kindly face.

"Vair the pine marten," said Dunstan, "is it your wish to stay in Watersmeet and belong here?"

"Yes, my lord Elder," swore Vair.

"And do you swear to work with us, help where you can, and defend our good name?" Dunstan continued.

"I do," said Vair.

Dunstan turned to the watching villagers. "Is there anyone who thinks that Vair should not be one of us? If so, let that animal give the reasons now."

Vair wondered nervously whether anyone would object because he had come with Ragnar, but none of the villagers spoke.

"Then, Vair, welcome to Watersmeet," said Dunstan, laying a paw on Vair's shoulder. "You're one of us now."

The villagers applauded; Vair thought that he would burst with pride as Kyria hugged him and Flora engulfed his paw in both of hers and shook it vigorously.

As the applause died away, Shadow reappeared, carefully carrying Sandor's sword. His eyes shone as he gave it to Vair.

Vair fastened his paw firmly about the hilt. "Well, Ragnar," he said, "my challenge stands. Are you going to answer it?"

A slow grin spread over Ragnar's face. He pulled off his scarlet coat and tossed it at one of the stoats. His sword scraped in the sudden silence as he drew it from its sheath.

"Yes, scum," he said. "I'll answer your challenge. I'll teach you to respect your elders and betters. And I'll show the rest of these fools what they can expect if they get in my way."

His sword raised, Vair retreated rapidly into the empty space of the village green, and the villagers formed a huge circle around him and Ragnar.

"Too late to run away now, scum!" Ragnar taunted him.

He hurled himself at Vair and slashed his sword down. Vair slipped sideways, avoiding the blow and catching Ragnar's blade on his own. Striking it aside, he lunged forward; Ragnar barely raised his sword in time to block Vair's blade.

The silver fox's face changed. Vair saw that he had realized he was facing a skilled fighter, not the cringing animal he had despised until now. He stepped back, and Vair followed, thrusting hard and looking for the weak point in Ragnar's defenses. His sword point ripped through Ragnar's shirt, but the fox retreated again before Vair could wound him.

Hoping for a quick victory, Vair pressed harder still. The fox's strokes were growing wilder, and it was easier for Vair to beat his blade aside.

As their swords locked, he said, "Surrender, fox! Surrender and go—I'll spare your life."

Ragnar laughed. Before Vair realized what he was doing, Ragnar sprang back and then forward again, coming low under the blades, and thrust out a hindpaw to trip Vair.

Caught off balance, Vair fell. Pain stabbed through him as he jarred his wounded shoulder. His vision blurred; he saw Ragnar as a threatening shadow poised over him, ready to strike him down. Shouts from the crowd pulsed in his ears. At the last second he gathered his wits enough to roll aside.

He had kept his grip on his sword. Coming to one knee, he brought the blade up in time to block Ragnar's blow. The fox stood over him, bearing down with all his strength. Vair knew that if he gave way now, he would die.

Slowly, bit by bit, he forced Ragnar's sword back until he could climb again to his hindpaws. He was beginning to feel tired, and the old wound was throbbing painfully. Sweat pricked his fur and trickled down into his eyes. Even though Ragnar must have been tiring too, Vair could see no sign of it.

Beginning to be desperate, he lunged forward. Ragnar sidestepped and brought his sword swinging around; Vair felt the point bite into his sword arm. As he recoiled, drops of blood spattered onto the grass.

"See, little scum?" Ragnar said. "I'm going to kill you, just like I killed your father."

Fury almost blinded Vair. With a yell of rage, he sprang forward, but Ragnar was not where he thought he was. His wildly slashing sword met nothing. He heard Ragnar's laughter. For the first time, he thought he was going to die.

Then Vair remembered the sunny afternoon at Coolspring and the practice bout he had fought with Sandor. He heard his father's voice saying, "If you're fighting, really fighting for your life, don't let your enemy make you angry. That's when you make mistakes."

It was as if a fresh breeze blew over him, cooling his brow and clearing his head. He was still angry, but now it was a cold and controlled anger. Vair took a deep breath, spun to face Ragnar as he attacked from the side, and blocked the blow that would have killed him.

Summoning all his skill, Vair pressed forward once again. Not overconfident anymore, he advanced step by step, pushing Ragnar back. Triumph faded into uncertainty in the fox's eyes. He was gasping for breath, as if the night spent drinking in the Merry Ferret was beginning to show at last.

Then Vair saw his chance. Ragnar raised his sword, leaving himself unprotected. Vair lunged and struck home; Sandor's sword blade sank into Ragnar's chest, and the fox fell. A choking cry came from him. Ragnar lay still on the sunlit grass.

Vair pulled out the sword and raised the blood-stained blade in a salute, as if somewhere Sandor were watching him. Then he let it fall. It was over; Sandor was avenged, and Vair hoped that now he could rest in peace.

Vair thought he could hear a roaring in his ears. Staggering from exhaustion, he dropped to his knees beside his dead enemy and put his paws over his face.

Vair the Hero

Kyria watched the combat in silence, her eyes fixed on the two battling animals. It was hard to watch her new friend Vair risking his life when she could do nothing. Shadow quivered with anxiety as he stood beside her, gripping her paw hard.

When the silver fox fell, there was a moment of silence as Vair raised his sword. Then a roar burst from the throats of all the watching villagers. They rushed forward.

"Come on!" said Kyria.

She ran toward Vair, and Shadow sped in front of her until he reached Vair's side.

"Vair—Vair, are you hurt?" Shadow asked.

Vair raised his head. To her relief, Kyria could see that he was smiling. "Not much. I'm all right."

"Keep back," Kyria said to the villagers who were crowding around Vair, congratulating him and wanting to shake his paw. "He's hurt. He needs rest and quiet."

"No, I'm really all right," Vair protested as she bent down to examine the slash along his forearm. He pulled himself to his hindpaws. "What about Gorm and the others? Where are they?"

Kyria had forgotten Ragnar's crew in the excitement of the fight. Now she looked around to see the huge ferret and the rest of them bunched together outside the Merry Ferret. One or two of them had their swords out, but they were shifting uncomfortably from hindpaw to hindpaw, as if none of them wanted to be the first to attack.

"There!" Kyria cried out angrily and raised a paw to point at the crew. "Are we going to let them ruin our village?"

"No!" All the villagers joined in a single shout. "Drive them out!"

They surged across the green. The bandits stared in disbelief and then broke for the cover of the forest with the villagers on their heels.

As the crowd streamed past her, Kyria saw Wiggin slapping at Ketch the stoat with a broom and shouting, "Spill my ale, would you? Take that!"

Captain Taffrail was slashing his sword at the tail of a fleeing rat, while Gorm the ferret was streaking along just behind them, eyes bulging with terror. Flora pounded after him, whirling her great two-handed sword around her head.

"Pussycat, am I?" she yelled. "I'll teach ye to call me pussycat! Stand and fight!"

Vair gripped his sword and looked as if he was going to join in, but Kyria grabbed his uninjured arm. "Oh, no, not you," she said. "You're coming home with me to have that wound seen to."

Vair looked as if he would protest but then stuck his sword blade into the ground and leaned on the hilt as he watched the bandits and their pursuers disappear into the forest. Some new arrivals, pushing carts or carrying bundles on their way to the fair, passed them on the edge of the trees and looked back in bewilderment, as if they couldn't figure out what was going on.

"I'd better talk to them," Kyria said. She was beginning to realize that their troubles were over at last, and the Fair could go ahead in peace. "Shadow, take Vair home, would you? And put some water on to heat. I won't—"

She broke off as Vair grabbed her arm. The pine marten was staring at the edge of the forest, where more newcomers were emerging. In a stifled voice he said, "Look."

Kyria saw a tall, slender pine marten pause on the edge of the trees to look around. She carried a small cub balanced on her hip, and another, older cub was at her side.

"Vair, is that . . .?" Shadow asked.

A smile of incredulous delight had spread over Vair's face. He stumbled forward; at the same moment, the little cub squirmed free of his mother and raced across the village green, squealing, "Vair, Vair!"

He hurled himself at Vair, and the two of them went rolling on the grass.

"Here, steady," said Kyria, hurrying to join them. "Vair's been hurt."

Vair and the cub were too busy hugging each other to notice. Kyria couldn't help smiling to see their happiness in being reunited. She turned to the older pine marten, who was hurrying across the green toward them, and held out a paw.

"Welcome to Watersmeet," she said. "You must be Vair's mother."

The pine marten clasped her paw warmly. "Yes," she said. "My name's Riska, and this is Mirra." The older cub bobbed a shy curtsey. "And this is Cuffi," Riska went on, bending down to detach her youngest cub from his big brother. "Cuffi, let Vair breathe, for goodness sake."

Vair got up and hugged his mother and Mirra. "I can't believe it," he said. "I can't believe you're all safe. How did you know where to find me?"

"We were on our way here," Riska explained, "because we hoped you might head for Watersmeet, or if not, someone might have heard of you. And then we met a bird."

"A big, fierce falcon!" Cuffi said. "He dived down—whoosh!—like that." He pounced on Vair's hindpaws with his claws extended like talons.

"Sir Peregrine," said Shadow. "He's always doing that."

"That's right," said Riska. "He said you were alive and we'd find you in Watersmeet, and that the Warden had sent him and some other birds to look for us."

"Of course!" said Vair. "Flick—the Warden—said he would do that."

"I must go and thank him," said Riska.

"Flick is my father," said Kyria. She introduced herself and Shadow. "Father might not be well enough to talk to you," she went on. "He—"

"Vair, you're hurt!" Riska interrupted, noticing Vair's wound for the first time. "What's going on?"

"I fought with Ragnar," Vair told her. "The silver fox who killed Father. You do know about Father?" he added.

Riska's face grew shadowed. "Yes. We went back to our camp to look for you, and we found Sandor there. We buried him beside the river."

"Vair took revenge for him," Kyria said. "Ragnar was making trouble here, too, and Vair fought him. He's the hero of the village."

Vair looked embarrassed, while Cuffi jumped up and down, cheering, and Mirra smiled admiringly at her brother.

Riska gave Vair another hug, and the shadow passed from her face. "Sandor would be proud of you," she said.

By now the other villagers were starting to reappear from the trees, congratulating themselves loudly and slapping each other on the back. Flora strode toward Kyria and the others, with a smug smile on her face. She was whistling softly through her teeth and cleaning the blade of her sword with a wisp of grass.

Kyria started to ask her what had happened to Gorm the ferret, but then decided that she really didn't want to know.

"Let's go home," she said. "Riska, you're all my guests. We've got a lot to talk about, and tonight is the Fair Feast!"

As the sun went down over the river, Shadow went home to his oak tree to fetch his flute. If he hurried, he thought, he might just have time to round up the choir for one more practice before the Fair Feast began and they had to perform.

The ladder leading to his veranda was still pulled up, but Shadow sprang easily up the tree trunk, humming contentedly to himself. Now that Ragnar and his crew were gone, village life could get back to normal, and there would be time to decide what they ought to do about the Horn of Eaglesmount.

When he let himself into his tree house, Shadow checked that the horn was still where he had left it, in his linen cupboard tucked between the folds of a quilt. With one paw he traced the strange lettering of the old language of the eagles, and wondered for the thousandth time what the Lord Owl meant to do with the horn if it ever fell into his claws.

Then, remembering the time, he covered the horn up again. Ignoring the unwashed breakfast dishes, he collected his flute from the music stand, along with the music for the Fair Feast in its birch-bark binder.

He let himself out again onto the veranda, closed the door behind him, and turned to find himself surrounded by owls.

At first, in his shock, Shadow thought there was a whole crowd of them; then he realized there were only three. Two were perched in branches of the tree, while the third clasped the veranda rail with fierce talons. One was completely white and seemed to shine with a pale glow. The second was brown, with a white breast

and a blank white face.

But it was the third owl who frightened Shadow most. He was huge, with dark tan feathers marked with black, and large, glaring amber eyes. Shadow remembered the Lord Owl that Vair had described, who had called the bandits together in the hills. A blast of pure evil seemed to come from him, terrifying Shadow more than his cruel beak and hooked feet.

Shadow's first instinct was to flee inside and bar his door. But as he hesitated, frozen with shock, the white owl glided down silently and thrust himself between Shadow and the tree trunk. As Shadow turned he was enveloped in soft wing feathers, half smothered, and then pushed across the veranda so that he stumbled to his knees in front of the Lord Owl.

"What do you want?" he asked the owl.

The Lord Owl unlocked one taloned foot from the rail and pointed it at Shadow. "Give me the horn."

"The horn? I—I don't know what you mean."

Soft, hooting laughter came from the owl on the branch above. The Lord Owl did not share in it.

"You lie, squirrel," he said. "You were seen last night —you and the pine marten and the falcon who thinks he knows so much. You had the horn then, and you have it now. Give it to me."

Shadow looked around desperately. Twilight was gathering, and here in the top of the tree, he was alone with the owls. All the other villagers would be gathering for the Fair Feast. There was no one who could possibly help him.

"Give me the horn," the Lord Owl repeated. "Or I'll rip you apart and take it."

Shadow shivered, but he managed to get to his hindpaws. "No," he said.

Shadow braced himself, expecting the crooked talons to tear into his chest. Instead, the Lord Owl poked his head forward, staring hard at Shadow. He found that he could not look away. He felt cold. His vision blurred as if dark mist were swirling in front of him, until all he could see was the amber glare of the Lord Owl's eyes. Shadow thought that he was falling, and he struggled to breathe. When the Lord Owl spoke, his voice seemed to echo from a great distance.

"You will give me the horn," said the Lord Owl. "You will give it to me now."

Fair Feast

The night was warm, and the moon rose round and silver above the roof of the Merry Ferret. A soft breeze carried the scents of summer over the village green. Long tables and benches for all the villagers and the traders who would be their guests for the Fair Feast had been set up there.

Kyria dusted her paws and looked with satisfaction at the tables. They were spread with white linen cloths and loaded with the best food that Watersmeet could provide: perch and fennel pie, mushroom bake, a whole pike stuffed with herbs, huge bowls of butternut squash soup, scones with beechnut butter, apple tarts and honey cakes, and bowls of candied nuts.

Flora came up from behind and clapped her paw on Kyria's shoulder. "It's a grand night, Kyria, and this is a grand spread ye're giving us."

"And we've something to celebrate," said Kyria, smiling. "Just imagine if Ragnar and his crew were still here!"

"They'll not be bothering us again," said Flora.

Wiggin hurried past them, pushing a cask of Barley Brew on a wooden cart, while two of his children, with long candles, began lighting the lanterns that hung from the trees. Traders were starting to appear down the path from the Fair Field, and the villagers were emerging from their houses.

"Flick's much better," Kyria went on. "He was conscious when I got home after the fight, and he managed to sit up and have some soup. But he'll have to rest for a long time before he gets his strength back."

"Like that, ye mean?" said Flora, cocking her head toward the steps that led up from the riverbank.

Kyria whirled to see her father, dressed in his best coat and seated in a chair that was carried along by Vair, Riska, and two strong young villagers. Mirra and Cuffi were walking alongside.

"Father!" Kyria strode across and planted herself in front of the chair so that Flick's bearers had to stop. "What do you think you're doing? You should be in bed!"

"The Warden of Watersmeet can't miss the Fair Feast." Flick's voice was weak and shaky, but he had the old gleam in his eye. "Don't worry, Kyria. I won't stay long. But I have a few things I want to say before the Feast begins."

"And I have a few things to say to you," Kyria retorted. "But they'll keep."

She stood aside and let Flick's bearers carry his chair to the center table and set it down beside the carved oak chair where Dunstan the Elder would sit. Already the animals were starting to take their seats, and a buzz of cheerful conversation broke out as traders greeted old friends they hadn't seen since the last fair.

Kyria took the seat beside her father, and Flora sat by her, nose twitching in impatience as she looked at all the good things spread in front of her.

"Where's the wee tree-rat?" the wildcat asked.

"Shadow? He said he was going home to fetch his flute. He's probably practicing," Kyria said as she looked around the village green.

"He'll miss the Feast if he doesn't hurry," said Flick.

Kyria raised her eyes. "He hasn't the sense of a horsefly. If he doesn't come soon, I'll go and look for him."

At that moment Dunstan the Elder appeared. He was wearing the shabby black coat that he had worn for more Fair Feasts than any animal could remember, and he fumbled in one of the pockets for a folded piece of paper with his notes scribbled on it.

Calling for silence by rapping on the table, he said, "Welcome, gentlebeasts. Welcome to you all. The Fair will begin tomorrow at sunrise, and I wish you all a prosperous and . . . um . . . happy time. The threat to our village is over, and—" Here he paused and gazed benignly around him over the tops of his spectacles while the villagers cheered. "And for that," he went on when the noise had died down, "we have to thank the newest member of our village, Vair the pine marten."

There was more cheering. Vair looked ready to crawl under the table with embarrassment, while Riska's eyes shone with pride and Cuffi bounced up and down, squeaking and clapping his paws together.

"We all hope," Dunstan went on when he could make himself heard again, "that this will be the beginning of a long and happy life for Vair in Watersmeet. And now,"—he peered at his notes again—"nothing remains for me to say except, enjoy the Feast!"

Wild applause broke out as Dunstan nodded and smiled and took his seat. Flick raised his voice to make himself heard. Kyria glared at him in case he had any ideas of standing up to speak.

"With your permission, Elder, there's something I'd like to say," Flick began. "I took a bad wound this morning, and although I'm getting better, I think my fighting days are over. I mean to resign as Warden."

Cries of protest came from the assembled animals, who were looking at each other with dismayed expressions. Kyria wanted to protest, too, but she kept silent. She had to admit to herself that her father was right. It would be a long time before he recovered his fighting strength.

"Warden, are you sure?" Dunstan asked.

"Quite sure," said Flick.

The old badger looked worried. "Then we'll need to elect a new Warden."

"We will." A broad smile spread over Flick's face. "And I have just the candidate." He glanced across the table to where Vair was sitting with his family. "Who could be better than the young fellow who saved us all today?"

Vair sprang to his hindpaws. He looked appalled. "Flick—sir—I can't be Warden. I . . . I'm too young for a job like that."

"Young or not, you're the bravest fighter I've ever met," said Flick.

"But I've only just joined the village," Vair argued.

"And you've done more for the village in that short time than many an animal who has lived here all his life," said Dunstan. "But we had better do the thing in the proper form and have an election."

He rose and rapped for silence again. "Friends," he

said, "we need to find a new Warden for Watersmeet. Flick has suggested Vair. Do any of you want to put forward another name?"

No one spoke.

"Then," Dunstan went on, "I declare that Vair is elected—if he agrees."

"Vair, you must," said Kyria. "We need you here."

Vair hesitated and then said, "In that case—yes. And thank you—thank you all!"

He looked dazed with happiness as the animals all erupted into cheering, banging the tables and raising their cups to drink to his health.

Flick leaned across the table to shake his paw. "We'll have a long talk tomorrow," he promised. "You'll need to take up your duties right away. There are always problems during the fair, but nothing you can't handle."

"And now," said Flora, "maybe we can get on with this feast. My stomach thinks my throat's cut."

Flora drew one of Mistress Wiggin's perch and fennel pies across the table and cut herself a huge slice. Kyria was pouring herself a cup of elderflower cordial when she felt a tug on her sleeve. She looked down to see one of the young rabbits from Shadow's choir.

"If you please, miss," he said, blinking anxiously, "we're supposed to sing soon, and we can't find

Shadow anywhere."

Kyria let out a sound of exasperation. "All right, I'll see to it." To Flora she said, "I've got to go and find that scatty squirrel. Save me a piece of that pie."

Flora looked up from her plate, mouth full of succulent perch, flakes of pastry on the end of her nose, and twitched her whiskers in reply.

Then, as Kyria rose to her hindpaws, she saw Shadow, rushing headlong across the village green, with his tail streaming out behind him. He came to a halt in front of the center table. His eyes were staring as if he had seen something that terrified him; he was gasping for breath and shuddering.

Vair, who was nearest, got up and went to him. "What's the matter?" he asked, putting an arm around the squirrel's shoulders. "What's happened?"

Shadow clutched at him. "Oh, Vair, it was terrible! And I couldn't help it, truly I couldn't!"

"Couldn't help what?" Kyria asked sharply.

Shadow caught his breath in a sob. "It was the Lord Owl," he said. "Oh, Vair, the Lord Owl has taken the horn!